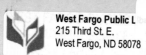

A MOTHER'S VOW

"Husband, hold up!" Winona suddenly cried, bringing her mare to a halt.

Nate drew rein and shifted in the saddle. He thought she had seen something, but it was only her parfleche. She had tied it down too hastily. The rope had loosened and the parfleche was flapping against the mare.

Hooves drummed. Ezriah joined them at last. More winded than his mount, he leaned on the saddle horn and said urgently, "Before you go any farther, there's something I haven't told you. You lit out before I could."

Winona's lips pinched together. "Wicked men have stolen Blue Flower. Nothing else matters."

"This might," Ezriah said. "Their leader, Killibrew, said he'd kill the girls if you tried to follow. I'd take him seriously, were I you."

"This from the one who let them take the children," Winona said scathingly. "We cannot let them get away," she added in a tone that brooked no dispute. Completing a knot, she lithely forked her animal. "Before this day is done my knife will drink their blood."

The *Wilderness* series:

#1: KING OF THE MOUNTAIN
#2: LURE OF THE WILD
#3: SAVAGE RENDEZVOUS
#4: BLOOD FURY
#5: TOMAHAWK REVENGE
#6: BLACK POWDER JUSTICE
#7: VENGEANCE TRAIL
#8: DEATH HUNT
#9: MOUNTAIN DEVIL
#10: BLACKFOOT MASSACRE
#11: NORTHWEST PASSAGE
#12: APACHE BLOOD
#13: MOUNTAIN MANHUNT
#14: TENDERFOOT
#15: WINTERKILL
#16: BLOOD TRUCE
#17: TRAPPER'S BLOOD
#18: MOUNTAIN CAT
#19: IRON WARRIOR
#20: WOLF PACK
#21: BLACK POWDER
#22: TRAIL'S END
#23: THE LOST VALLEY
#24: MOUNTAIN MADNESS
#25: FRONTIER MAYHEM
#26: BLOOD FEUD
#27: GOLD RAGE
#28: THE QUEST
#29: MOUNTAIN NIGHTMARE
#30: SAVAGES
#31: BLOOD KIN
#32: THE WESTWARD TIDE
#33: FANG AND CLAW
#34: TRACKDOWN
#35: FRONTIER FURY
#36: THE TEMPEST

#37
WILDERNESS

PERILS
OF THE
WIND

David Thompson

LEISURE BOOKS NEW YORK CITY

Dedicated to Judy, Joshua and Shane.

A LEISURE BOOK®

August 2002

Published by

Dorchester Publishing Co., Inc.
276 Fifth Avenue
New York, NY 10001

ISBN: 0-8439-5043-9

The name "Leisure Books" and the stylized "L" with design are trademarks of Dorchester Publishing Co., Inc.

Printed in the United States of America.

Visit us on the web at www.dorchesterpub.com.

PERILS
OF THE
WIND

Foreword

Enjoyed by millions, Wilderness *is the longest-running Mountain Man series published today, an exciting saga that chronicles the adventures of the King family and their close friends. The Kings had a cabin high in the Rockies, in an area now occupied by Estes Park, Colorado, long before the tide of settlers arrived. They were one of the first to brave the untamed frontier, and their struggles and heartbreaks make for stirring entertainment.*

The book you hold in your hands, like all those before it, is based on the journals of trapper Nate King. Many of his entries are quite detailed and require little embellishment. Others are no more than hastily scribbled notes. The latter applies to the story you are about to read. In his journal entry Nate King wrote: "My daughter and the other girl have been taken. We are off after them at first light, and may the Almighty look with mercy on those who are to blame because I sure as hell will not."

Fortunately, the author was able to locate a secondary source. It will be detailed at the end of the narrative.

Chapter One

Evelyn King was only eleven, but she was old enough to know that when the forest fell suddenly quiet, it was a bad sign. Her father, Nate, had taught her much woodlore; her Shoshone mother, Winona, had added to her store. So when all the birds in her vicinity stopped chirping and a red squirrel in a nearby pine abruptly stopped chattering, she gripped the arm of her companion, put a finger to the girl's lips, and whispered, "Don't make any noise, Melissa. Something's not right."

Melissa Braddock glanced around in confusion. She was almost three years younger and four inches shorter. Her fine sandy hair, clipped short at the shoulders, was only a few shades lighter than the faded brown homespun dress she wore. "What do you mean?" she blurted, louder than she should.

Evelyn had to remember to be patient with her new friend. As her mother had pointed out a few days earlier, Melissa hadn't spent her entire life in the wilderness, as she had. Nor had Melissa ever lived among Indians, as the Kings did every year during their annual get-together with the Shoshones. She was, as Evelyn's father put it, a "babe in the woods."

"Hush!" Evelyn whispered. "Hunker and listen." Pulling Melissa down beside her, she cocked her head from side to side. It was a trick her pa had taught her for detecting faint sounds.

"What's out there?" Melissa softly asked. Fear had crept into her face, and she looked like a scared rabbit set to bolt.

"I don't know yet." Evelyn was glad they were in high weeds. Her green dress, which was almost the same hue as the green eyes she had inherited from her father, blended in perfectly. Absently swiping at a stray bang of her raven hair, she turned into the breeze.

"Maybe we should run for it," Melissa suggested.

"Will you *please* be quiet," Evelyn said. The smaller girl didn't seem to realize the potential danger. The wilderness was filled with grizzlies and mountain lions and other hungry beasts, and while her pa had exterminated all the meat-eaters in their valley, from time to time new ones drifted in. Then there were hostiles to worry about, the Bloods and Piegans and Blackfeet and others who delighted in counting coup and taking scalps.

Melissa didn't know how to do as she was told. "Why don't we run for the cabin?" she insisted.

Evelyn shook her head. They were halfway around the lake and had a lot of open ground to cover. If something or someone was out there, they wouldn't get far. She strained her ears but heard nothing to explain the unnatural quiet.

"At least you have your gun," the chatterbox said.

Evelyn didn't say anything. Her small rifle, custom-built by friends of her pa's, the Hawken brothers in St. Louis, was only .31-caliber. For dropping small game it was just dandy, but it wouldn't stop the likes of a griz.

Another minute of awful stillness went by. Melissa fidgeted and gnawed on her lower lip, as nervous as a chipmunk when a bobcat was abroad. "Are we going to squat here all day?" she whispered.

"Be patient." Evelyn had learned long ago that a person could never be too careful. In her eleven years she had seen a lot of people die, whites and Indians alike. Some had died in battle, some had been victims of disease. A few had passed on of old age. And then there were the dozens slain by wild beasts, her least favorite way to die.

Some were indelibly impressed on Evelyn's mind. There was the Shoshone who had been gored by a bull buffalo, for instance. It had been during the Heat Moon, the month of July, when vast herds filled the prairies. A dozen warriors had gone on a surround, and Laughs Loud, a kindly man who once gave her some honey to eat, was thrown from his horse when it stepped into a prairie dog hole. Before he could climb back on, a bull charged, hooked a horn in his belly, and ripped him wide open. Laughs Loud had been brought back to the village on a travois and somehow lived until sunset.

Evelyn remembered standing there, staring at a spreading dark stain on the blanket someone had covered him with. At one point, Laughs Loud's wife had lifted the blanket to vainly apply a poultice, and Evelyn had glimpsed jagged rib bones laid bare and his intestines slowly oozing from his abdomen.

The worst, though, had been a white man mauled by a silvertip. Palmer was his name, and he had been off picking berries when he spooked a cub. Its mother came roaring out of the underbrush and proceeded to bite and tear at him in a frenzy. He was clinging to life by a thread when he was brought to the rendezvous site. Her father had gone over to see what the ruckus was about and she had innocently tagged along, never dreaming what she would find.

Palmer was a ruin. Half his face was missing. The rest had been partially caved in by a mighty blow, and his eyeball had popped out and was dangling over his ravaged cheek.

Whole chunks of flesh had been shredded from his body. His right shoulder, right arm, and right thigh were exposed down to the bone. His left arm had been mangled, his left leg half bitten off. Blood sprayed from a gash in his throat every time he breathed. He lingered long enough to request word be sent to his wife back in Ohio.

Small wonder Evelyn had no desire to be torn to ribbons by a bear or other animal. Melissa could gripe to high heaven, but Evelyn wasn't about to budge until she was sure it was safe. She shifted to the left, away from the lake, and stiffened at the faint scrape of a stealthy tread.

"I'm tired of squatting here," Melissa grumbled. "I want to go back. I'm hungry, and your mother baked all those cookies for us this morning. Let's go have some." She started to rise.

"No!" Evelyn grabbed the younger girl's wrist and yanked her back down. "There's someone out there!"

"Are you sure?" Melissa cast wide eyes at the heavy growth.

The *crack* of a dry twig confirmed it. Evelyn spied a darkling shape off in the pines, prowling toward them.

Melissa had seen it too, and was trembling like an aspen leaf in a chinook. "How do you know it's not a deer or an elk?" she whispered.

"They don't walk on two legs," Evelyn responded. That much she could tell. Since everyone else was back at the cabin, whoever was stalking them had to be a stranger, and a stranger often spelled trouble. It might be a scout for a hostile war party. Gripping Melissa's hand, she said, "We'll have to move fast. Stay by me."

"What do you have in mind?" Melissa wanted to know.

Evelyn had two choices. They could loop westward along the shore to the trail that linked the lake to her family's homestead, but to do so they had to pass uncomfortably close to the figure in the trees. Or they could head for the east end of the lake and work their way completely around.

It would take a lot longer, but it promised to be a lot safer and that's what counted.

Melissa dug her nails into Evelyn's hand. "He's coming closer!"

The vague shape was skirting a thicket not forty feet from where they were concealed. Evelyn had to decide, and she had to decide quickly. She moved eastward, tugging on Melissa when Melissa balked, her Hawken in her other hand. Only if she had to would she resort to the rifle; it only held one shot, a shot that would be folly to waste.

Evelyn stayed in a crouch. Every few yards she glanced back. Apparently, the figure in the trees hadn't spotted them. With a little luck they'd reach a cluster of boulders ahead and duck into them unseen.

Then Melissa sneezed. Not a tiny sneeze, either, but a sneeze worthy of a moose or an elk.

Evelyn was dumbfounded. Hoping against hope that the skulker hadn't heard, she glanced toward the figure and saw that it had pivoted in their direction. "Light a shuck!" she directed, and gave her companion a shove.

Bleating in dismay, Melissa stumbled onto one knee and would have pitched onto her stomach had she not thrown both arms out to check her fall. "What did you do that for?" she complained.

"Don't just lie there," Evelyn said, slipping a hand under the other girl's arm. *"Run!"* She gave her another push.

Melissa looked over a shoulder, spied the shadowy shape now hurrying purposefully toward them, and bolted like a mountain goat being stalked by a cougar. "Shoot him! Shoot him!" she bawled.

Evelyn did no such thing. She paced the younger girl, wishing for a clear view of their pursuer. Her pa had taught her that she must never discharge her weapon unless she was absolutely sure of her target. A wounded man, like a wounded beast, could be twice as dangerous. "Better to go for a kill with your first shot," her father cautioned her,

6

"than to have a riled grizzly or an enraged hostile out for your hide."

Melissa dashed into a gap in the boulders and flattened against a slab of rock. The whites of her eyes were showing and the color had drained from her face. "What are you waiting for?" she demanded. "Do you want us to end up like my folks?"

The reminder helped Evelyn better understand the younger girl's fright. It wasn't all that long ago that Melissa's entire family—mother, father, and siblings—had been wiped out in a savage clash with marauding members of the Blackfoot Confederacy. Melissa had witnessed their final moments, and ever since had been prone to horrible nightmares that snapped her awake, screaming and crying, in the middle of the night.

"We don't know who it is yet," Evelyn said.

"So? They're after us, aren't they?" Melissa looking longingly at the Hawken. "If you don't have the nerve to do it, give your gun to me."

Evelyn wasn't about to. She doubted the smaller girl could shoot all that well, for one thing. For another, her parents had made it plain she was to never, ever give her rifle to another person unless she knew and trusted them completely. And while she liked Melissa, Evelyn couldn't say with all honesty that she trusted her to do what was best.

"Well?" Melissa urged. "Do something!"

"Keep quiet," Evelyn said sternly, and craned her neck to the end of the slab for a look-see. The figure was gone. She scoured the woods and the high weeds, but it was nowhere to be seen. Either the man had run off, which was unlikely, or he was sneaking up on them. Straightening, she scanned the boulders and the tall trees beyond.

Melissa caught on that something was amiss. "What is it? Where did they get to?"

"I don't know," Evelyn said. As the oldest and most experienced, it was up to her to find out. She edged past Melissa and peered past an oval boulder pockmarked with holes the size of small coins. The wall of undergrowth offered no clues.

"We can't just stand here!" Melissa said.

"Do you have a better idea?" Evelyn countered. Since the stalker couldn't get at them without being spotted, they were safe enough for the moment. She gazed out over the lake, its tranquil, shimmering surface sprinkled with geese, ducks, and brants. To the west a slender column of smoke rose into the afternoon air. Her mother was getting an early start on supper. Her father, as she recollected, was shoeing his bay in the corral. A shot in the air would bring him on the run. But it would take a minute to reload, and whoever was in the nearby woods might attack. Except for her bone-handled knife, she would be defenseless.

"I don't want to die!" Melissa declared.

"Who does?" Personally, Evelyn would love to live to a ripe old age and die in bed, as her great-grandmother was supposed to have done. But odds were she wouldn't if she stayed on the frontier.

Melissa jabbed a finger to the north. "There! I saw something move!"

So did Evelyn. Whether it had been their stalker or a branch waving in the breeze was impossible to say. She trained the Hawken on the spot, but no one appeared. Suddenly Melissa began to cry, sniffling loudly as tears streaked her cheeks. "Cut that out," Evelyn said. She wouldn't be able to hear if the man tried to slink closer. "What in the world is the matter with you?"

"I'm afraid."

"That's no excuse to blubber like a baby," Evelyn said in mild disgust. As her pa had stressed over and over, the key to surviving in the wilds was to keep calm in a crisis. Those who gave in to brain-numbing fear were the ones who be-

8

came worm food. In the belief that Melissa would be braver if she were armed, Evelyn drew her knife and held it out, hilt first. "Take this. Just in case."

"In case what?" Melissa swiped at her nose with a forearm. "You expect me to stab someone?" She didn't bother to reach for it. "I'm just a girl."

"What does that have to do with anything?" Evelyn didn't regard being female as some sort of handicap. Her mother was every bit as courageous and capable as her father, and could kill when the occasion called for it. "When your life is at stake, you do what you have to."

Something struck the slab behind them with a loud retort. Evelyn and Melissa both spun, and Evelyn saw a small stone that had bounced off the slab and was rolling to a stop. The man in the trees had thrown it! He was trying to spook them, she deduced, and it had worked. Melissa started to quake again, worse than before.

Evelyn shoved the knife into its sheath and started to turn. Only then, when she heard the pad of onrushing feet, did it occur to her that the rock had been meant to distract them. She had made a grievous mistake. She tried to whirl in time, but an arm looped around her waist and she was hoisted into the air as if she weighed no more than one of her rag dolls.

Melissa screamed.

A high-pitched cackle pealed in Evelyn's ears, and a voice that crackled like gravel in a tin pot howled, "I did it! I got the better of you, sprout, fair and square!" Evelyn was swung in a circle, then deposited lightly on her feet. "Wait until I tell your ma! It'll teach her to always go on so about how savvy you are!"

Anger coursed through Evelyn's veins, anger so potent she almost reversed her grip on the Hawken to use it as a club and bash the prancing dervish in front of them. "Mr. Hampton!" she exclaimed. "You shouldn't go around scaring folks like that!"

Ezriah Hampton paid her no heed. Laughing merrily, he danced an energetic if ungainly jig. He was well on in years, his hair and beard as white as driven snow, his face as wrinkled and seamed as old leather. When he was excited, as now, his right eye had a habit of twitching uncontrollably. His left eye was gone, lost long ago to an Indian lance, and in its place had grown a stitch-work ridge of scar tissue.

"My pa won't take kindly to what you've done," Evelyn scolded.

Ezriah stopped dancing and scowled. "I never took you for a tattletale, girl." He put his hands on his scrawny hips. "Did I tell on you that time you swiped a bunch of cookies without your mother's permission?" Standing there in his loose-fitting purple shirt, buckskin pants, and red velvet coat, he looked almost comical. Over the coat hung a blue cloak, the collar trimmed with white lace. Knee-high black boots served as his footwear.

"I didn't swipe them, exactly," Evelyn replied. "Ma said I could help myself."

"To one cookie, not four," Ezriah said. "She didn't want you spoiling your meal, remember?" He had a rifle slung across his back, and two large flintlocks tucked under a leather belt inlaid with silver studs. In an ornate scabbard on his right hip hung a curved sword with a fancy hilt. His most prized possession, though, was one he never let anyone touch: a large, finely tooled leather bag attached to his belt behind the scabbard. "So if you tell on me, missy, I'll squeal on you."

Melissa had stopped crying. Resentment replaced her fear, and she boldly marched up to Hampton and smacked him on the leg. "Scaring us like that was mean! If I was older I'd thrash you."

"What a pair of grumps," Ezriah said. "All I did was have a little fun. You'd think the two of you would be grateful." He jabbed a thumb at Melissa Braddock. "Especially you.

10

You've been sulking around with a long face for pretty near two months."

"Can you blame her?" Evelyn came to the younger girl's defense. "She lost her whole family."

"I lost mine a coon's age back," Ezriah argued, "but you didn't hear me whimpering and carrying on like she's been doing. I learned to accept it, to live with it, just like she has to do." He draped a hand on Melissa's shoulder, but she jerked aside and glowered. "Suit yourself, girl," he chided. "Just don't expect a hug on those nights when the devil comes to haunt you."

Evelyn stiffened, adopting the same posture her mother did when her mother was mad. "That's enough. If all you came out here for is to scare and badger us, you can save yourself the trouble." The old-timer had a knack for getting her goat. Next to her brother, who used to tease her mercilessly, Hampton was the most annoying man she'd ever met.

"Now, now," Ezriah said good-naturedly. "Don't work yourself into a snit. I saw you two leave the cabin and thought you'd like some company." He pushed his broad-brimmed Spanish-style hat back on his head. "The truth is, girl, I'm bored silly. Sitting around watching your pa and ma make cow eyes at one another ain't exactly my notion of entertainment." Ezriah sighed. "I can't wait to get back to civilization. All those years I was held captive, I hear it's changed quite a bit."

Evelyn could imagine how he felt. Until recently, Hampton had been a hostage of the Sa-gah-lee, a remote tribe who dwelled deep in the mountains. His outlandish wardrobe had been taken from other hostages, unfortunates with no further need for clothes. "It won't be long," she commented. "Another month or so, at the most."

"I can't wait." This from Melissa, who had dried her eyes and nose. "Uncle Orson was always my favorite. I'm going

11

David Thompson

to live on his plantation and have my own pony and everything. He promised me in his letter."

"I'm bound for New Orleans," Ezriah said. "I hear it has more taverns and bawdy houses than most ten cities, and I aim to carouse and—"

"What's a bawdy house?" Melissa asked.

"Eh?" Ezriah regarded her as if she were a creature he had never set his good eye on before. "How's that, child?"

"What's a bawdy house?"

The old man glanced at Evelyn. "Why don't you enlighten her?"

Evelyn had heard the expression only once before, used by a half-drunk trapper at a rendezvous. Her father had socked him on the jaw and told him not to talk about such things in the presence of children. So while she had no idea what a bawdy house was, she suspected it was one of those adult things her parents were forever telling her she would learn about when she was older. "How would I know? What *is* a bawdy house?"

Ezriah puffed out his cheeks like an agitated chipmunk. "Hellfire and damnation. You're eleven years old and your folks ain't told you what lips are for? My God, in my day girls were married off by fourteen. You're practically a spinster."

Evelyn was about to ask what he thought lips were for, but Melissa spoke first.

"You shouldn't swear all the time, Mr. Hampton. My ma used to say swearing is the hallmark of the feeble-minded."

"Let me guess, child. Your mother was a Bible-thumper who believed in living right and never used a naughty word?" Ezriah smiled thinly. "People like her always give me an ache in my backside. They go through life with blinders on, like those nags that pull carriages in big cities back east."

Melissa's eyes narrowed. "Did you just call my mother a horse?"

12

"If the reins fit," Ezriah quipped.

"Mean, mean, mean," Melissa said, and without warning she stepped up to the old trapper and kicked him full in the shin.

Evelyn laughed when Hampton howled like a coyote and commenced hopping about on one foot while clasping the other leg in pain. "It serves you right," she said between giggles. "It's not nice to insult folks."

"Shows how much you brats know!" Ezriah sputtered, as red as a sunset. "I was explaining how things are, is all." Hobbling to a boulder, he leaned against it and rubbed his hurt limb. "Calling a black bear black ain't hardly an insult."

Melissa moved toward the lake. "I don't want to talk to you anymore," she told him. "Not until you say you're sorry."

Evelyn went with her. Runoff from a score of pristine peaks that hemmed the valley kept the lake full year-round, its waters crystal-clear and deep. Sinking onto a knee, she dipped a hand in and raised it to her mouth to savor a sip when her gaze happened to fall on an imprint in the soft soil. It was a track, a human track left by a full-grown man. "Look at this!" she declared, her thirst forgotten.

Melissa failed to appreciate its importance. "Your pa has been over this way. So what? He goes hunting all the time."

"Pa didn't make it," Evelyn said, tracing the outline with a finger. "See here?" She tapped the heel. "This was a boot." Her father wore moccasins crafted by her mother. As best she could judge, the print had been made sometime within the past couple of hours. The toes pointed eastward, toward the mouth of a stream fed by the lake.

Ezriah limped over, still rubbing his shin. "What's all the fuss about?" he inquired, and leaned over Evelyn's shoulder. "Well, well. We've got a visitor. A white man, too." He unfurled and moved toward the stream. "Let's track him."

"We should go tell pa," Evelyn advised.

"A few minutes more won't hurt," Ezriah said. "Least-wise, to give us some idea of where the fellow went."

Evelyn hesitated. Her parents had instructed her not to trust strangers until strangers proved themselves trustworthy, and she had learned the hard way over the years that her folks had a good reason. Many of the men who roamed the mountains, white and red alike, were men of evil intent. Men motivated by wicked hearts and violent desires, men to be shunned at all costs. "I don't think we should," she objected.

"Then run on home to Momma," Ezriah taunted. "I'll only be a few minutes."

Melissa hadn't moved either. "Why bother?" she said. "Whoever it is, he's probably long gone by now."

She was wrong.

Evelyn saw the old trapper stop and glance sharply to their left. Lifting her head to a low knoll, she beheld four men. Hardcases, her father would call them. The kind of men she had just been thinking about.

Chapter Two

Ezriah Hampton knew they were in danger the moment he laid his good eye on the quartet on the knoll. He had always had a talent for reading people, and the foursome were trouble with the bark on. Their largely cold, humorless expressions, their flinty, arrogant gazes, branded them as rogues in whom decency had never taken root. To deceive them, he plastered a smile on his puss and casually draped his right hand on the butt of one of his smoothbore pistols. "Howdy, gents," he crowed, halting in midstride. "We bid you a hearty welcome."

None of the four acknowledged his greeting.

On the right stood a hulking bear of a brute in grimy buckskins and a raccoon hat that had seen a lot better days. A bushy brown beard framed a rough-hewn face weathered by years spent out-of-doors. Like the others, he was armed to the teeth, with a rifle, a brace of pistols, and a butcher knife.

Next was a half-breed, part Pawnee by the looks of him. His hair had been shaved except for a spiked crest down the center. He had angular, bony features, including a hooked nose bigger than an eagle's beak, and he wore a breechclout and moccasins. Red ocher had been smeared on his chest and face. Of the four, his features were the most inscrutable; he was a marble slate with finely sculpted sinews.

The third man was shorter than the rest but twice as wide. None of his bulk appeared to be fat. He was a human wall of muscle and gristle capped by a ruddy moon face that bore the scars of several fights—notably, a jagged knife wound that hadn't healed properly, leaving him deformed. His left cheek and the corner of his mouth sagged an inch or so lower than the right side. A wispy mustache and beard did little to alleviate his grotesque image. His attire consisted of a faded flannel shirt and dirty pants, a floppy black hat, and badly scuffed black boots. Oddly, he now smirked, as if at a private joke.

On the left stood a lean willow who favored a clean chin and clean buckskins. His guns were newer than those of his companions. He was the youngest, not much over twenty, and of the four of them, he was the only one who had behaved halfway friendly and smiled at Evelyn and Melissa.

"Got wax plugging your ears, gents?" Ezriah said amiably, moving so he was between the newcomers and the girls. He had to get them out of there, but they couldn't just turn and run. The four would easily overtake them. "Or did the Comanches get their paws on you and rip out your tongues?"

The bearded giant on the right finally broke their silence. "Gabby cuss, isn't he?" he remarked sarcastically.

The short man's smirk widened. "Ugly cuss, too."

Ezriah never liked having his affliction, as he called it, made light of. Bristling, he snapped, "You're a fine one to talk, mister. Taken a gander in a mirror lately? You're enough to give these kids nightmares."

The short man's twisted mouth curled in a crooked smile lent a sinister air by the fiery spite that flared in his ferret eyes. "For an old cuss you've got a lot of nerve."

"And a lot of weapons," Ezriah said, patting his pistol to stress his point.

"Was that a threat, old man?" rumbled the man on the right.

Ezriah was about to say, *Hell, yes!*, but he held his tongue. He had the welfare of the girls to think of. So he lied. "Hell, no. Just an observation, is all." Assuming a fake smile, he gestured toward the west end of the lake. "You boys look a little peaked to me. You must be hungry. Why don't you come up to the King place and give your corns a rest? Nate King doesn't mind strangers stopping in." He deliberately mentioned his friend by name. King's reputation as a formidable frontiersman had spread far and wide, and might deter the quartet from misbehaving. "Maybe you boys have heard of him?"

"Nate King," the short man said, staring at the smoke rising above the far trees. "Who hasn't? They say he's killed more grizzlies than any jasper alive."

"That's the one," Ezriah said, grinning. His little ploy had worked. Now the foursome would think twice before starting something.

"They also say he's friends with most every tribe in these parts," the young willow piped in. "The Shoshones, the Crows, the Flatheads, even the Utes."

Evelyn stepped up alongside Ezriah and proudly declared, "That he is. My ma is Shoshone, and they adopted my pa into the tribe."

The short man's eyes narrowed. "So you're King's brats, are you?"

"I'm not a brat!" Evelyn said angrily. "I'll thank you not to call me names, mister, if you know what's good for you."

Ezriah put a hand on her shoulder and gently squeezed, thinking she would take the hint and shush up. But no such

17

David Thompson

luck. The girl had a temper, and once her dander was up she was a regular wildcat.

"My pa doesn't like rude people and neither do I. Who are you, and what are you doing in our valley?"

"Just passin' through," the short man said. At a nod from him, all four came down the knoll.

Ezriah felt Evelyn stiffen. She was a bright tyke and had realized her mistake. "Why don't you and Melissa go fetch your folks?" he casually suggested so the strangers wouldn't become suspicious.

"Hold on a second, girl," the short man said as Evelyn started to turn. "Before you run off, I'd like you to answer a few questions."

To Ezriah's dismay, Evelyn paused. Melissa hadn't caught on to the fact that they were in peril and was standing there like a stump, smiling warmly. Ezriah wanted to bean her with a rock. He settled for motioning to her to head back, but she was too fascinated by the newcomers to notice.

"How about if you introduce yourselves first?" Evelyn said. "That's the polite thing to do."

"Perish forbid we shouldn't be polite," the big bear replied, and chortled. "I'll do the honors." He touched a thick, dirty finger to his barrel chest. "I'm Bittner. The 'breed, there, is called Haro. It's not his full name, which is longer than the Mississippi and as hard to say as Greek." Bittner nodded at the young willow. "That there is Kyle. He's from Maryland—"

"Tell them our life's story, why don't you?" the short man curtly interrupted. "My name is Killibrew. Yu could say I'm the leader of this bunch, in that what I say goes." He looked at the others to see if anyone refuted his claim, but no one did. "Now that we've been all gentlemanly-like, girl, how about you return the favor? What's your handle?"

Evelyn told him.

Ezriah was in a quandary. The four men were slowly spreading out without being obvious about it. Clearly, they intended to get around behind to keep them from leaving. But he didn't dare say anything to Evelyn or Melissa or the four might go for their guns. He had to keep on smiling and pray to high heaven he had the four pegged wrong.

Killibrew studied Evelyn intently. "We heard tell you have an older brother who doesn't think kindly of whites. Did we hear correctly?"

"Zach used to be like that," Evelyn admitted, "but ever since he married and moved out, he's not as hotheaded as he used to be."

"So he doesn't live hereabouts anymore?" Killibrew said. "Interestin'." He winked at Bittner. "It's just your folks up at the cabin, is that it?"

Ezriah jumped in before Evelyn could reply. "Not quite. Several of his friends from his trapping days are staying over. Maybe you've heard of them too. Shakespeare Mc-Nair, Scott Kendall, and Simon Ward." He saw Killibrew frown, and inwardly giggled at his cleverness.

At that juncture Melissa stepped forward. "I didn't see any other people at the cabin today," she declared. "When we went for our walk, no one was there but Mr. and Mrs. King."

Killibrew's frown curled upward. "Is that so, girl? Only the Kings?" He pursed his lips. "Why, old-timer, it sounds to me as if you've been pullin' our leg. You wouldn't do that, would you?"

Ezriah tried to make light of Melissa's blunder. "You know how kids are. Always playing games. She saw them. She's just teasing."

"I am not," Melissa said.

Kyle and Haro were almost past Ezriah. They were trying to be nonchalant about what they were up to by pretending to be interested in the woods, in the lake, in the sky, in anything and everything except the girls and him. Ezriah's gut churned. Dropping a hand onto Evelyn's and Melissa's slim shoulder, he said, "How about if we prove it to them?

We'll take them back so they can see for themselves."

Killibrew suddenly scooted forward. "Not so fast. The oldest girl still has a few questions to answer." The smile he bestowed on Evelyn was as oily as castoreum. "Is it true your pa pays a lot of visits to Bent's Fort?"

"We go there every other month or so for supplies and whatnot," Evelyn said. "My ma is partial to the trade goods. My pa likes to jaw with Mr. St. Vrain and some of the others. Me, I like the hard candy." Smiling sweetly, she reached across Ezriah and clasped Melissa's hand. "Come on. It's time we were going. Ma will want our help with supper."

Ezriah had to hand it to her. They almost succeeded. Killibrew was rooted in bafflement for a few seconds as Evelyn pivoted and strode for home.

Kyle shot a glance at the leader, awaiting instructions. It was the breed who quickly stepped in front of the girls, his rifle held in the crook of an elbow, the muzzle a hand's width from Evelyn's head.

"What do you think you're doing?" she demanded.

Haro arched a thin eyebrow at Killibrew, who chuckled and walked up behind them. "We can't have you rushin' off on us. It wouldn't be hospitable. Our camp is over yonder"— he jerked a thumb at the knoll—"and we'd be honored if you'd join us for a cup of hot chocolate."

"I don't want any, thank you," Evelyn said.

Melissa, however, was like every other child. "Hot chocolate? I'd love some, Mr. Killibrew. It's one of my favorites in all creation."

Ezriah molded his right hand to the flintlock. Four-to-one odds weren't to his liking, but he was determined to hold the foursome at bay until the girls made their getaway. Then he saw Bittner, saw Bittner's rifle centered on his abdomen. The big man grinned and shook his bushy head. Ezriah had no choice but to slide his hand off his pistol.

Killibrew had grasped Melissa's arm and was steering her toward the knoll. In her youth and innocence she offered no resistance. "Come along. All three of you. We have enough for everyone."

Evelyn balked. Her Hawken was at waist height, and for a few nerve-tingling seconds Ezriah thought she would bring it to bear.

Haro intervened, his rifle muzzle practically brushing Evelyn's neck as he grasped the Hawken's barrel and eased it from her grasp. She glanced at Ezriah, and he smiled encouragement. Evelyn had made the right decision. The 'breed would surely shoot her dead if she fought back, and she was smart enough to know it.

Bittner wagged his long gun at Ezriah. "Didn't you hear Killibrew?" he goaded. "We'd like for you to join us a spell."

Ezriah was mad enough to spit quartz. The young one, Kyle, also had a rifle pointed in his direction, so there was nothing for it but to continue smiling like an idiot and fall into step next to Evelyn as she trudged up the incline.

"Sorry," she whispered. "I should have acted sooner."

"Blame Melissa if you're going to blame anyone," Ezriah said. "She doesn't have the brains the good Lord gave a turnip."

"She's young yet," Evelyn whispered.

Until that moment Ezriah hadn't given much thought to the age difference between the two, but now that he did, he had to concede that Evelyn was much more mature. He opened his mouth to say so.

"What's all the whispering about?" Bittner inquired, tramping along a few feet to their rear. "If you've got something to say, speak up so the rest of us can hear."

Ezriah muttered a few swearwords.

Approximately fifty feet into heavy timber on the other side of the knoll was a glade. Four horses were tethered in a string, their saddles and packs arranged around a crackling fire. A fire so small it gave off virtually no smoke. A battered coffeepot perched on an old tripod over the crackling flames.

Killibrew led Melissa to a folded blanket and bid her sit. She showed more teeth than a politician on the stump as he rummaged in a pack and fished out a tin. "Here we go," he said, showing her the lettering on the top. "Chocolate, just like I promised."

The tin, Ezriah observed, was new. So was a tin cup Killibrew removed from the pack next. "You've paid a visit to Bent's Fort yourselves recently, haven't you?" he asked. Located on the Arkansas River, the fort was the only trading post within hundreds of miles. It wasn't a military installation, although its builders, brothers Charles and William Bent and their friend Ceran St. Vrain, had the foresight to erect towers at the southeast and northwest corners large enough to accommodate field pieces. During the heyday of the beaver trade it had done a bustling business in plews. Now it was a leading supply center, as well as the social hub of the central Rockies. Mountain men went there not only for provisions but for all the latest news on everything from doings back in the States to the latest tribal conflicts.

"We have a long ride ahead of us and needed to stock up," Killibrew was saying. He dipped into the pack once more and this time retrieved a piece of hard candy the size of a walnut. "How would you like to suck on this while we're waitin' for the hot chocolate to heat up?" he asked Melissa, who cheerfully accepted.

"We really should be going," Evelyn said. "My folks will be worried if we're not back soon, and my pa will come check on us."

"I doubt that very much," Killibrew said. "But if he does, Haro will let us know."

Ezriah looked over his shoulder. The half-breed had melted into the vegetation as silently as a specter. Bittner and Kyle were at the glade's boundary, each with a thumb on the hammer of his rifle. "You'd better hope you're right. Her father won't take kindly to what you've done. Nor will her mother, for that matter."

"To offerin' these kids some refreshment?" Killibrew said, and smiled thinly. "Don't fret yourself over Nate King. We're not yacks. We've asked around. We have things well in hand."

"What is this all about?" Ezriah bluntly asked. "What do you hope to gain?"

"We'll get to that in a bit." Killibrew bent over the tripod and opened the tin. "I had just put the pot on to make coffee when we heard your voices." Pinching some of the ground chocolate between his thumb and forefinger, he added enough to the water to suit his taste. He didn't waste a grain. Chocolate was expensive, a luxury few could afford.

Melissa slurped away at the candy like a piglet guzzling slop. "This is the best sweet I've ever ate, Mr. Killibrew," she said. "My ma wouldn't let me have candy much. She said it was bad for my teeth."

"A smart gal, your mother," Killibrew said. "I never had one to speak of. She walked out on me when I was seven, and I've been fendin' for myself ever since."

"What about your pa?" Melissa asked.

"He was a riverboat gambler. Never wanted anything to do with her or me. He died in a knife fight when I was nine." Killibrew patted a dagger sporting an ivory hilt, nestled on his left hip. "This was his. The only thing of his I own." Drawing it, he held the polished double-edged blade so it reflected the sunlight, inches from Melissa. To Ezriah and Evelyn he said, "Why don't the two of you make yourselves comfortable? Set down your hardware and pick a spot near the fire."

"You want me to put down my rifle?" Evelyn said.

"Please," Killibrew said, casually moving the dagger nearer to Melissa's throat. "You can't drink with your hands full."

Ezriah shifted and saw Bittner and Kyle taking steady aim, Kyle at him, Bittner at Evelyn. Any pretense at civility had been discarded. Never for a second did he doubt they

23

would shoot. He might be able to drop one, but the other would surely core him or the girl, and he couldn't abide the idea of harm befalling Evelyn. He'd never come right out and say so, but he'd grown rather fond of her over the past several months.

Evelyn fingered her Hawken in indecision. A chip off the parental block, she had her mother's feistiness and her father's nerves of steel.

Ezriah wouldn't put it past her to put a slug in Killibrew in the belief she could drop him before Killibrew cut Melissa. Tapping her shoulder, he nodded toward the other two vermin. "Maybe we should do as he wants, runt."

Defiance lit her young countenance, but Evelyn slowly lowered the Hawken to the grass and reluctantly let go.

"Now you and your armory, old man," Killibrew said, sliding behind Melissa and dipping the tapered tip of the dagger to within a whisker of her skin.

Ezriah's sense of outrage climbed by leaps and bounds. He had done his share of despicable deeds. More than his share, some might say. But he had never stooped to threatening children, and would no sooner harm one than he would a woman or a kitten. Well, women, at any rate. He hated cats.

"Sometime this year would be nice," Killibrew said.

Ezriah slipped both flintlocks from under his belt and deposited them on the ground. His knife was placed beside them. Last was his rifle, and it was all he could do not to snap it to his shoulder and shoot Killibrew dead.

"Don't forget your oversized pigsticker."

The sword had been among an enormous assortment of weaponry collected by the Sa-gah-lee over a span of centuries. Ezriah had been dazzled by its burnished bronze hilt and flawless curved blade. That blade now scraped against the scabbard's lip as he drew it out and reverently lowered it. "Keep your greasy fingers off this or I'll have your heads."

Killibrew snickered in mild contempt. "You're a hoot, old-timer. A goat your age shouldn't make threats he can't carry out. Keep it up and I'm liable to take you over my knee." He made as if to replace the dagger, then paused. "What's in that leather bag? A derringer, maybe?"

"My possibles," Ezriah said. Every mountain man worthy of the name carried a bag or pouch containing odds and ends they might find useful: flints and steel for making fires, whetstones for sharpening knives and axes, needles for sewing, and more.

"Open it."

Ezriah would rather have the few teeth he had left pried from his mouth with pliers. Weapons and clothes weren't the only thing the Sa-gah-lee had collected. They had also amassed an incredible amount of money, coins mostly, of various mintage. From early Spanish and French to some minted within the past decade. To the Sa-gah-lee they were no more than pretty baubles. To Ezriah they had been the promise of a whole new life, and before leaving the city of the Elders, he had crammed the leather bag with a small fortune. It had to weigh upward of twenty pounds, but he would sooner part with his life than give it up. He was on the verge of refusing to let Killibrew look at it when fate came to his aid.

Haro materialized out of the thin mountain air and announced in clipped, accented English, "A woman yells at the other end of the lake. The mother, calling her children."

"I told you," Evelyn declared. "My pa will be out searching for us soon, and you'll have a heap of explaining to do."

Killibrew accepted the news with disturbing calm. "I suspect he just might, girl. Fair enough. Bittner, you and Kyle saddle up and throw the young ladies on your horses so we can get the hell out of here. Haro, saddle my horse, will you, while I watch our friends?"

The three men rushed to comply, and Killibrew palmed a pistol and pointed it at Ezriah. "As for you, old man, you weren't part of the plan."

"What plan?" Evelyn asked, and was ignored.

Bittner bent to heft a saddle. "Shoot him as proof we mean business. Then leave a note for the Kings."

"What if it makes Nate King mad?" Kyle interjected. "Remember those stories they told us at the fort? Why not have the old man deliver our terms instead?"

Killibrew's brow furrowed, and for a few moments he was deep in thought. "That's not a bad idea, boy. No sense in rilin' King any more than he will be." He winked at Ezriah. "Guess what? You get to be our messenger, whether you want to or not."

The three other men hastened to the horses. In short order they mounted and kneed the animals to the middle of the glade, Haro leading Killibrew's by the reins. Bittner brought his sorrel up close to Melissa, leaned down, and forked her into his brawny arm. She yelped and struggled to break free, but she was vastly overmatched.

Kyle extended a hand toward Evelyn. "Now it's your turn, little miss," he said pleasantly enough.

"I'd rather be shot," Evelyn retorted.

Killibrew swiveled his pistol toward Melissa. "Would you rather she was shot, too? I won't be trifled with, girl, not with so much at stake." He cocked the gun. "Either you do as I damn well tell you, or so help me I'll send her to her Maker right here and now."

Ezriah admired how quickly Evelyn decided, and how bravely she permitted Kyle to swing her up behind him. "Harm either of those kids . . . ," he said, and left the statement unfinished.

Killibrew backed toward his dun. His flintlock never wavered as he gripped the pommel and forked leather. The others headed into the trees to the northeast, but he lingered, saying, "Tell Nate King we have his brats. Tell him that unless he brings us four saddlebags full of gold, he'll never set eyes on them again."

Amazement washed over Ezriah. "Who the hell do you think he is? John Jacob Astor?" At one time Astor had been the wealthiest man on the continent. "Where the hell is he supposed to get it?"

"From his Injun friends," Killibrew said in all earnestness.

"You're loco," Ezriah flatly responded.

Killibrew shook his head. "No. I'm canny as a fox. You see, we overheard that St. Vrain feller mention how King paid for the last supplies he bought with a poke full of nuggets. So we nosed around some and learned he's done it before. A dozen times or better, one clerk told us."

Ezriah was immensely skeptical, to say the least. "If Nate had that much gold, I'd know. I've nosed all around his cabin and been over every square foot of this valley."

"Who says it has to be anywhere nearby?" Killibrew countered. "The rumor at Bent's Fort is that his Injun friends showed him a stream way back in the mountains where nuggets are thicker than ticks on a coon dog."

"If that were true, why haven't the Indians spent it themselves?"

"Some have. A while back, a Cheyenne buck brought in a chunk of ore as big as my fist. Before that, it was a Shoshone." Killibrew's moon face was a mask of raw greed. "All that talk got my pards and me to thinkin'. We're tired of livin' hand to mouth. We'd like to go back east and have a fine mansion and carriages and servants to wait on us hand and foot."

"Who wouldn't?" Ezriah said without thinking.

"Exactly. So you tell Nate King he has three weeks. We'll be waitin' for him on the Missouri River."

"Where, exactly?"

Killibrew laughed. "Do you take me for a simpleton? Directions are waitin' for him at Bent's Fort." He bent toward Ezriah. "It's important you convince him I mean what I say, old man. If he doesn't bring the gold, the girls die. If he doesn't show on time, the girls die. If he comes after us instead of going for the gold, the girls die. Make sure he understands." Lashing the reins, Killibrew wheeled his horse and galloped off.

Ezriah Hampton watched until the kidnappers were lost from view. Then he squinted up at the sky and sighed. "Been sleeping on the job again, I see?"

Chapter Three

The man chopping wood was well over six feet in height, broad of shoulder and narrow at the hip. His movements possessed a fluid pantherish quality that hinted at enormous strength and vitality. He was stripped to the waist for the task, and corded muscles rippled in the sunlight with each powerful swing of the heavy ax. The *chop-chop-chop* of keen steel biting into a downed sapling rang with the precision of a ticking clock.

Nate King believed in planning ahead. It was only early fall, but already some of the leaves were starting to turn color and most mornings and evenings were uncomfortably chill. When winter arrived, with its periodic snowstorms and temperatures plummeting well below zero, he intended to have a mountain of firewood stacked close to his cabin, enough to see his family through to next spring.

Nate always put the welfare of his loved ones before all else. Daily, he diligently strived to do all he could to make their lives better and safer. There were always chores to do, always work of some kind that needed doing. The life of a settler was one of unending toil, the life of a mountain man doubly so.

Hunting occupied a lot of Nate's time. Keeping food on the table was no simple feat, as it had been in the early days when game in the valley was abundant. In the intervening decades he'd slain most of the elk and deer, and those that remained were naturally wary and consequently more difficult to track down and shoot. Often he had to venture into neighboring valleys or high up on adjoining slopes to find game.

Still, Nate considered the valley a literal paradise on earth. It was *his* valley, his own private domain, carved out of the wilderness at the cost of much physical labor despite repeated and sundry threats to life and limb. Grizzlies, marauding painters, packs of wolves, and bands of hostiles had all menaced his paradise at one time or another, and had all been slain or driven off.

In recent years the number of incidents had declined. The last grizzly had visited the valley two winters previous. Wolves hadn't posed a problem in ages. And the Utes, who for the longest while tried to make worm food of him, had agreed to a truce and now left him and his in peace and quiet.

Nate enjoyed the relative tranquillity. He was pushing forty, and his favorite pastime was to sit in front of the hearth in the evening reading one of his many books while his wife knitted or sewed and his daughter played with one of her many dolls. The sense of wanderlust that had brought him to the frontier had faded with the years. He was content. He was happy. What more could a man ask of life?

Nate never regretted his decision to leave New York City, never regretted giving up a budding career as an accountant to trek to the Rockies in search of adventure and excitement. He shuddered to think he might have spent the rest of his days chained to a desk, scribbling in ledgers from dawn until dusk. By now he would have been hopelessly old before his time, grossly overweight, and probably wearing spectacles.

Pausing, Nate lowered the ax and inhaled the crisp mountain air deep into his lungs. He was caked with sweat, and the air tingled his skin. He gazed out across his valley, at the smoke curling from his spacious, sturdy cabin, at his corral and the half-dozen horses milling about in it, and he smiled with pride. Not bad for a former accountant. Not bad at all.

Nate also became aware of his wife shouting his daughter's name. It dawned on him that she had been calling for some time now and there had been no answer. Scooping up his buckskin shirt from the stump on which it lay, Nate hurriedly shrugged into it while hastening to the corral and on around to the front of the cabin. The front door was wide open. His wife was across the clearing, at the head of a well-worn trail that led down to the lake. The sight brought him up short—and brought another smile to his face.

Bathed in a shimmering shaft of sparkling sunlight, Winona was breathtakingly beautiful. Her flowing black tresses, spilling past her shoulders, shone with a lustrous sheen. And even though she had borne two children and for years endured the travails of an arduous life, she was as enticingly slender as a woman half her age. Her normally smooth features creased in concern, she cupped her hands to her rose-hued lips and shouted in Shoshone, "Blue Flower! Where are you? Answer me!"

Blue Flower was their daughter's Shoshone name.

Nate came up behind Winona without being heard and startled her by gently wrapping his free arm around her waist and nuzzling her neck. "Problems?" he said. It wasn't uncommon for their youngest to go traipsing off about the valley and stay away longer than she was supposed to. Evelyn had an independent streak a mile wide.

Winona switched to English and said in exasperation, "She was supposed to be back half an hour ago."

"She took her rifle, didn't she?" Nate had few ironclad rules, but that was one of them. No one was to stray far without a firearm.

"Yes. They were only going to take a short stroll along the lake. Ezriah went after them, but he hasn't returned." Winona put her hands on her hips. "I swear, husband. Sometimes I think she does this just to annoy me."

"You sound like my mother," Nate mentioned, chuckling, and received a poke in the ribs. "If there was trouble, we'd have heard a shot," he assured her. Still, he was never one to take anything for granted. "I'll go see what's keeping them." Nate headed inside.

"Tell her I do not appreciate being kept waiting," Winona said, following. "Melissa and her were to help me bake a pie."

"You know your daughter," Nate said. "She'd rather gallivant than work. She must get that from your side of the family." For his jest he received another jab, low in the back, and he laughed.

"I bet Ezriah is to blame," Winona said. "He is worse than she is. Always going off to explore and poking his nose where it doesn't belong. Remember that cave they found? And the black bear?"

Stepping over the threshold, Nate laughed louder. The oldster and the girls had been exploring a slope to the south, in the shadow of Long's Peak, and stumbled on an opening in the rock wall. Ezriah thought it might lead to a cave, so he'd squatted and was about to stick his head in when he came chin-to-chin with a black bear. It wasn't much more than a cub, but it gave him a terrible fright. He'd squawked and fallen on his backside, and the bear had bolted on by, squealing up a storm.

"It is regrettable the bear didn't bite his nose off," Winona remarked.

"Now, now," Nate said softly as he leaned the ax in a corner. The oldster was an ornery cuss and could get a rise out of her without half trying. The same with Evelyn. The truth be known, Nate suspected that Ezriah secretly enjoyed raising their hackles. Ezriah wasn't happy unless he was arguing with someone, and he was happiest of all when he was arguing with females.

Nate slid his ammo pouch and powder horn from pegs on the walls and slung them across his chest. He already had a Bowie in a beaded sheath on his right hip. A flintlock pistol went on either side of his brass belt buckle. Last of all, he retrieved his Hawken from the mantel over the fireplace, then gave his wife a peck on the cheek. "I'll have them back before you know it."

"Unless they're halfway to St. Louis," Winona said dryly.

The sun was warm on Nate's back for the few seconds required to reach the trail. Shadows closed over him as he broke into a run. On either side heavy foliage hemmed him in. He had been meaning to clear most of it out; cougars were unduly fond of lying beside game trails and springing on unwary prey as it went by, and the big cats didn't care whether the prey was four-legged or two-legged.

The trail sloped gradually downward, emerging on the lake's north shore. Once in the open, Nate surveyed the lake from end to end but failed to spot anyone. Obviously, Evelyn had gone her own merry way.

Nate examined the ground. A pair of small, fresh-as-could-be tracks showed where the two girls had ambled eastward along the shoreline. He paralleled them, holding to a steady, mile-eating jog worthy of an Apache. Another set of prints, left by Ezriah's peculiar high-heeled boots, confirmed that the old man had gone after them.

Out on the placid lake swam a bevy of geese, their long necks curled into question marks. Ducks quacked noisily and fluttered their wings, or dipped their bills in the water after fish. The mallards always gave Nate a chuckle. They

33

had a habit of upending and floating with their hind ends straight up.

Soon the tracks Nate was shadowing diverged. The girls had gone on along the shore, but Ezriah had veered into the vegetation. Nate could guess why. Hampton was an inveterate practical joker; next to arguing, the old-timer most loved to play tricks on people. A week ago Ezriah had caught a toad and put it in the bread box. When Evelyn opened it, the toad had hopped out, giving her a fright and causing Hampton a fit of convulsive mirth.

Nate came to where his daughter and Melissa had stopped and turned toward the trees. When they moved on, the lengths of their strides indicated that they had been running. He trailed them to a cluster of boulders and found where Ezriah had caught them off guard. From there the tracks drew him to the lake.

Suddenly Nate halted. His pulse quickened. Someone else was in the valley! He counted two, three, four new sets of tracks. One was a man who wore flat-soled boots, and whose short stride hinted at a corresponding stature. Another wore moccasins with stitching reminiscent of the Pawnees. The other two wore store-bought hunting boots available at any general store or trading post. Alarm filled Nate. Strangers had caused his family no end of trouble.

The prints filed toward a knoll, and as Nate sped toward it he heard the crunch of a footfall and glanced up to find Ezriah Hampton, looking as glum as glum could be. Hampton was holding his rifle in one hand and Evelyn's Hawken in the other.

"There wasn't anything I could do, hoss."

"Ezriah?" Nate said, his alarm rising. He dashed up the knoll and gripped the older man by the arms. "Where are the girls?"

"The bastards had me covered the whole time. I'm sorry. Sincerely sorry."

34

Anxiety lanced Nate. He dashed down the other side and on to a grassy glade. A small fire smoldered at its center. Footprints and hoofprints were everywhere, the tracks jumbled one over the other. As he studied them, Ezriah approached.

"There were four of them, Nate," the older man said forlornly. "They took your daughter. They took Melissa."

Nate spun, his head awhirl with terrible images. "Why?" was the foremost question. His fear for his daughter was so overpowering, he could virtually taste it.

"The idiots think you're rich. They've kidnapped the girls for ransom." Ezriah pointed to the northeast. "They went that way. They can't have more than a ten-minute start. If we hurry—"

"Tell me as we go," Nate said. Grabbing Hampton by the elbow, he raced toward the lake. It would take five minutes to reach the cabin, another five to saddle up. In under a quarter of an hour they could be hard in pursuit.

Nate was moving so rapidly, Ezriah was hard-pressed to keep up. "They caught us by surprise," he said, huffing and puffing. "Their leader is an unsavory sort named Killibrew. They'd heard about you paying for provisions at Bent's Fort with gold, and they want to exchange the girls for four saddlebags full."

"I don't know any Killibrew," Nate said. Which wasn't unusual. In recent years more and more cutthroats had been drifting into the Rockies, shiftless brigands who lived by hook or by crook and made life miserable for honest settlers and mountaineers.

"There are two other whites and a 'breed," Ezriah revealed. "Were you to ask my opinion, I'd say he's the most dangerous of the bunch. They usually are."

Nate didn't reply. It was generally held that half-breeds were notoriously savage, their violent natures the result of the mix of blood that went into their makeup. Whites and Indians alike tended to look down on them, a fact that had

35

caused Nate's son no end of grief. Evelyn, being a girl, was spared the brunt of the widespread prejudice, but she still received bitter looks from time to time from pilgrims at Bent's Fort and elsewhere.

"I tried to tell them they were crazy," Ezriah said, "that you're not as rich as old King Midas. But they wouldn't believe me. Killibrew thinks you know of a secret stream somewhere in the high country where nuggets can be plucked like dandelions."

"He does, does he?" They were moving at a brisk pace, but not fast enough to suit Nate, so he increased his speed. Every second was crucial. By the position of the sun it had to be after four. Another couple of hours and the sun would set, and with it any hope of overtaking the kidnappers before nightfall. He shuddered to think of Evelyn and Melissa in the clutches of the cutthroats all night long.

The trail head seemed impossibly far away. Nate chafed at every yard they covered, and when they finally came to the trail he flew toward the cabin as if his ankles were imbued with wings. Bursting into the clearing, he raced toward the corral and shouted to Winona, who was waiting in the doorway.

"The girls have been taken!"

Winona never said a word. She didn't scream or collapse in hysterics, as some women might have. She disappeared inside, and in less than two minutes she was back out again, bearing a rifle and pistols and toting a pair of parfleches crammed with supplies. By then Nate had saddled his big bay and was throwing a blanket onto her mare.

Ezriah cringed when Winona bestowed a withering glance. Flipping a saddle onto a horse, he said apologetically, "I don't blame you for being mad at me, Mrs. King. But I did the best I could."

Nate filled his wife in while tightening her cinch. He tied one of the parfleches behind his saddle, stepped into the stirrups, and was off down the trail at a trot.

"Wait for me!" Ezriah bawled. "I ain't quite done!"

Nate had no inclination to slow up. Nor did Winona, who trotted alongside him as soon as they reached the lakeshore. Side by side they galloped eastward to the knoll and on over it to the glade.

The shadows were lengthening. Thankfully, the four men had made no attempt to conceal their sign, and Nate forged on at breakneck speed, indifferent to the risk to himself and the bay. When next he glanced back, Ezriah had caught up within a hundred yards and was gamely holding his own.

Winona's face was a blank slate, but Nate could imagine the torment she must be suffering. Mothers and daughters always shared a special bond. Evelyn was Winona's literal pride and joy; to lose her would be devastating.

Nate consoled himself with the thought that Evelyn was smart for her age and had remarkable grit and spunk. She could handle herself with the aplomb of a fifteen-year-old. Melissa was another story. She was nowhere near as level-headed. Still miserable from the loss of her family, she had been moping around the cabin for weeks. Only in the past couple of days, after Nate received an answer to a letter he'd sent her kin in North Carolina, had Melissa shaken off her doldrums and begun to enjoy life again. She was keenly anticipating the arrival of her favorite uncle in another month, and going to live with him on his plantation.

A low limb shattered Nate's reverie. Ducking low, he whisked underneath it with a needle's width to spare. He turned to warn Winona, but she had spotted it and lithely swung onto the side of her mare, Comanche style.

They said little. There was no need. They both fully realized the gravity of their daughter's predicament—and the price of failure.

The kidnappers had ridden to the northeast for over four miles, hugging wooded slopes crowned by regal peaks mantled in pristine white. Nate was intimately familiar with every square foot of his valley, and the whole time he was winding along the base of the mountains, he racked his brain, trying to deduce where the kidnappers were headed. It had to be *out* of the valley. That much was certain. And in that case, they had to use one of the passes.

Nate knew of eight: two to the south, two to the west, three to the north, and one to the east, where the stream descended into the foothills. The eastern pass wasn't far from the glade. Logically, that was the pass they should have used, yet they hadn't. Which begged the question? Why not?

Of the three passes to the north, the nearest was in a defile high on the barren slope of a needle-point peak. From up there the kidnappers could see for miles in all directions and study their back trail for pursuit.

The next pass, on the next mountain over, could be reached only after hours of laborious climbing. Every foot of the way was forested, so the kidnappers could reach it undetected.

Or was it the third pass? Nate had used it many times on visits to his mentor, Shakespeare McNair, and to his son, Zach, who had moved out not all that long ago and had a homestead of his own in a virgin valley a lot like Nate's. The third pass was at the lowest elevation and thus was the easiest to reach. But it was the farthest.

Which would the kidnappers pick? Nate wondered. With his knowledge of the terrain, he could shave miles and save a lot of time if he guessed correctly. He knew of shortcuts the kidnappers couldn't possibly know about. But if he guessed wrong, if he chose the wrong pass, Killibrew's bunch would gain a great lead.

"Husband, hold up!" Winona suddenly cried, bringing her mare to a halt.

Nate drew rein and shifted in the saddle. He thought she had seen something, but it was her parfleche. She had tied it down too hastily. The rope had loosened and the parfleche was flapping against the mare.

Hooves drummed. Ezriah joined them at last. More winded than his mount, he leaned on the saddle horn and said urgently, "Before you go any further, there's something I haven't told you. You lit out before I could."

Winona's lips pinched together. "Wicked men have stolen Blue Flower. Nothing else matters."

"This might," Ezriah said. "Their leader, Killibrew, said he'd kill the girls if you tried to follow. I'd take him seriously, were I you."

"This from the one who let them take the children," Winona said scathingly. "We can not let them get away," she added in a tone that brooked no dispute. Completing a knot, she lithely forked her animal. "Before this day is done, my knife will drink their blood."

"Thirsty knife you've got there," Ezriah joked, and when it elicited a glare, he swiftly went on. "You're not thinking straight, lady. Yes, your girl is in danger, and yes, those mangy no-accounts need to have their wicks blown out, but they have one advantage we don't."

"What would that be?" Winona asked.

"They have the girls."

Nate was impatient to ride on, but the old trapper's words had planted a seed of apprehension. Men coldhearted enough to steal children were coldhearted enough to murder them. Yet the mere thought of not going on was unbearable. His soul was wrenched both ways, and he let his wife decide. "It's up to you."

"Need you ask?" Winona said, and gave her mare a smack.

Half an hour passed uneventfully. The tracks wound to the bottom of the mountain with the needle-point peak; the kidnappers were making for the barren slopes on high.

Nate shielded his eyes from the sun's glare and swept the mountain for movement. He was rewarded with the sight of riders half a mile above. Four horses, strung out in single file, picking their way toward the summit. "There they are!"

Winona shielded her eyes and uttered a rare oath. "They will reach the pass long before us."

"I'd be more worried about them spotting us," Ezriah commented. "Killibrew doesn't strike me as someone we should trifle with. He was quite specific. Nate is supposed to go to Bent's Fort for directions on how to deliver the gold—"

"You never told me that," Nate cut him off.

"Excuse me all to hell. I've had other things on my mind. Besides, you two didn't exactly let any grass grow under you. You were gone before I could saddle up." Ezriah's good eye twitched like a worm on a hook. "Let's quit quibbling and get on with it. But don't say I didn't warn you."

Winona assumed the lead. Her long black hair flying, she started up the lowest slope.

"I get the impression she's a mite peeved at me," Ezriah commented.

So was Nate, although he refrained from saying so. He couldn't help thinking that if the situation had been reversed, if he had been with the girls instead of Hampton, things would have turned out differently. He would gladly have given his life in Evelyn's defense, and taken as many of the kidnappers as he could with him. Meekness had never been his strongest trait. In the wilderness, turning the other cheek was a fatal flaw guaranteed to earn the cheek-turner a dirt nap.

The slope steepened, the climb requiring all of their attention. A single lapse might result in a spill and injury to both horse and rider. To the west the blazing sun dropped by degrees to the rim of the world, a fiery coal about to extinguish itself. Purple dusk slunk across the valley like a thief out to steal the light.

Nate lost sight of the kidnappers, but their tracks were still plain enough. More so since their mounts had cascaded stones and dirt in a steady rain, just as his own was now doing.

Ezriah, as was his wont, chattered on like a chipmunk. "When we catch up to these polecats, I want first crack. I owe them for playing me for a fool. They're all a slice off the same rancid bacon, and should be buried like all rotten meat."

Nate tried to shut the old-timer out, but it was like trying to shut out the constant sigh of the wind or the rustle of the dry grass.

"They talked big, but they're small and yellow and few to the pod," Ezriah waxed eloquent. "If I were ten years younger, I'd have pummeled them to a pulp and pissed on their remains. There was a time when I was considered a pretty formidable fellow."

"With your fists or your tongue?" Nate asked over a shoulder, and was treated to a barrage of profanity that put his wife's earlier oath to shame.

"Wait until your turn comes," Ezriah upbraided him. "One day you'll wake up to find your hair gray, half your teeth gone, and your muscles as puny as wet noodles. You'll lie in bed with tears in your eyes, wondering how God can be so cruel."

"It's called old age," Nate said. "It happens to all of us eventually."

"Listen to the philosopher," Ezriah retorted. "Do you want to know what old age really is? It's the Almighty's way of punishing us for our uppity attitudes when we're younger. We strut around like bantam roosters, thinking we have the world in our palms, but we're fooling ourselves. Our health goes, our minds fade, and we die as we were born, weak and helpless and not having any damn idea what's in store for us next."

"Now who's the philosopher?" Nate said when Hampton paused. After that the oldster was silent.

The trees thinned, the grass ended, and by midway up the mountain they were in the open, exposed to view from the rocky ramparts far overhead. Nate swore he could feel un-

David Thompson

seen eyes marking their progress, watching them every foot
of the way. He regretted being impetuous, and fretted that
by not listening to Ezriah they were sealing their daughter's
fate.

The slopes grew steeper, but Winona never slowed. Her
chin chiseled in relentless iron profile, she goaded the mare
on, indifferent to its welfare and her own.

Sapphire shadows blanketed the lower elevations. Most
of the sun was gone, its reign relinquished to a rising sliver
of moon. Soon stars would mushroom and the firmament
would darken. A sinking sensation in his heart, Nate was
forced to concede that overtaking the kidnappers before
nightfall was impossible. He looked up to say as much to
his wife and abruptly drew rein so the bay wouldn't collide
with her mare.

Winona had stopped and was sitting as rigid as a board,
the back of a hand pressed to her mouth as if to stifle a
scream.

Nate glanced past her, seeking what she saw, and an icy
sensation spread over him from head to toe.

An isolated tree framed the next rise. Starkly silhouetted
against the sky, suspended by the neck from a rope, was
one of the girls.

Chapter Four

Nate King's heart leaped to his throat. Slapping his moccasins against the big bay, he galloped past his transfixed wife and barreled up the rise. The slope was almost vertical and the bay began to slip and slide, unable to keep its footing. In frantic fear, Nate threw himself from the saddle and scrambled higher like a madman, levering himself with his left hand, his right holding the Hawken. The small form at the end of the hemp was shrouded in murky shadow and he couldn't tell whether it was Evelyn or Melissa.

A wail tore from Winona. Glancing back, Nate saw her spring from the mare. Ezriah was gaping in horror-struck bewilderment, too stupefied to move.

A tiny voice in Nate's mind screeched, *Please don't let it be Evelyn! Please don't let it be Evelyn!* A twinge of conscience afflicted him, but she was his daughter and Melissa wasn't. Like any parent, his first and paramount concern was for his own offspring. He liked Melissa, he cared for Melissa, but he loved Evelyn with the breadth and depth of his entire soul. She was as essential to him as life itself.

Tears gushed, blurring Nate's vision, and with an angry snarl he shook his head and swiped at his eyes with a sleeve. He had another ten feet to go. Talus rained from under him as he surged higher. Trying to stay upright was akin to trying to run on ice. His left leg suddenly pumped out from under him, and he jammed his elbow against the ground so as not to pitch onto his face.

"Evelyn!" Winona cried, clawing at the earth in berserk misery. "Evelyn! Evelyn! Evelyn!"

Nate had seldom seen his wife lose her self-control, but she had lost it now. She was beside herself with grief. Within seconds she was at his side. Together, they covered the final stretch and heaved up onto the rise. Shock brought them to a stop a yard from the rope.

It wasn't Evelyn. It wasn't Melissa. The kidnappers had taken Melissa's dress, slid it over part of a bundled blanket, and looped the rope around the top. The illusion had been quite effective.

Winona mewed like a kitten, shuffled to the effigy, and placed a hand on it, saying softly, "I have never been so glad of anything in my life, husband." She quietly wept, her whole body trembling from the intensity of her emotion.

Nate's legs were weak. His knees wobbling, he stepped to the tree and leaned his back against it. "Damn them," he said softly. "Damn them all to hell." It was unspeakably cruel, and was further proof, as if any were needed, that the men he was dealing with were devoid of scruples and decency.

Dirt rattled, and over the edge came Ezriah, huffing and puffing as if he had run five miles. He drew up short, his good eye focused on the effigy, and blurted, "Well, I'll be. Deucedly clever of the devils, wouldn't you say?"

"They are all going to die," Winona proclaimed. Yanking her knife out, she elevated her arm and angrily slashed at the rope. The abomination fell with a thud at her feet. She picked it up, unraveled the noose, and pulled out the piece of blanket wadded in the dress.

"It was a warning," Ezriah said. "Their way of telling us if we push on, if we don't abide by their rules, they'll do as they threatened." He sighed. "That's that, then. We'll have to turn back."

"Not on your life," Winona growled, shaking the blanket as if it were one of the kidnappers and she were throttling him. "I will not rest until Evelyn is in my arms." She moved toward the slope.

"No," Nate said.

Halting, Winona wagged the dress at him. "No? After what they have done! What else would you have us do?"

"Exactly what they want." Nate hated to admit it, but Hampton was right. He nodded at the high cliffs that flanked the pass. "They're up there right this moment, spying on us, waiting to see what we'll do. If we keep going, the next time it will be Evelyn or Melissa hanging from a rope."

Indecision contorted Winona's features. Love and common sense fought for mastery, and common sense won. Tears slipped from the corners of her eyes as she glumly nodded. "I just cannot bear the thought of our daughter in the hands of such vile men."

"Do you think it's any easier for me?" Nate rejoined. He stepped out from under the tree and put a hand on her shoulder. "I'd give anything to have them back safe and sound."

Ezriah cleared his throat. "For what it's worth, I think the kidnappers will do their best to keep the girls alive so long as they think they'll get their gold." He gave Nate a meaningful glance. "Gold you don't have."

Nate surveyed the heights. His decision to go back might cost his daughter her life. But it was the wisest move under the circumstances. "Tomorrow morning Ezriah and I will head for Bent's Fort. Winona, you'll stay at the cabin and—"

"I am going with you."

In the twenty years they had been man and wife, Nate had grown to know her as intimately as he knew himself. Her expressions, her posture, often held significance others missed. At the moment, lurking in the depths of her eyes was an indomitable resolve that brooked no argument. He could talk himself hoarse and it wouldn't make a difference. "All right. The three of us."

In silence they descended to their horses, mounted, and reined around. Midway down, Ezriah commenced to whistle to himself but stopped at a look from Winona that would wither a cactus.

Nate tried not to think of Evelyn and Melissa and how it must be tearing them apart to see Winona and him ride off. He trusted Evelyn would understand and would keep her wits about her until they were reunited. "I'm sorry, little one," he said, gazing at the craggy summit. "Please forgive me."

Evelyn King watched her parents and Ezriah Hampton wind down the mountain and fought down an impulse to cry. She refused to show weakness in front of her captors. They would only tease her, as Killibrew and Bittner had been teasing Melissa, and she refused to give them the satisfaction.

"There they go!" Killibrew cheerfully exclaimed. "I told you it would work, boys. Nate King might be the bull of the woods as far as some folks are concerned, but so long as we have his girls, he'll do whatever we want."

"It's the Shoshone I'm worried about," Bittner said. "What if she sics her kin on us? I'm rather fond of my hair."

"Why do you think we asked Haro to join?" Killibrew responded. "He's one of the best hunters and trackers in these parts. If any Injuns try to sneak up on us, he'll spot them long before they can get within arrow range." Killibrew grinned at the half-breed. "Ain't that right, Pawnee?"

Haro grunted.

Kyle was holding the horses by the reins. "I'm glad the plan worked. But I still don't see why we had to cut up one of my blankets instead of one of yours."

"That's what you get for being the youngest and the newest, boy," Killibrew said. "It might have been fairer to flip a coin, but I'm plumb out of coins." Laughing at his own wit, Killibrew walked to his mount. "Don't stand there like a bunch of dead trees. There's still enough light for us to make it through the pass. We'll camp on the other side and head for the meeting place at dawn."

"What's your rush?" Bittner asked. "It'll take King quite a spell to gather up enough gold. He won't show until the three weeks are up."

"Spoken like a simpleton who has never had kids," Killibrew said mockingly. "For all you know, King might have enough already, stashed somewhere. Either way, he'll move heaven and earth to save his precious little missies, and get to us as fast as he can." He winked at Evelyn. "Isn't that true, dearie?"

Evelyn clamped her mouth shut. She had never despised anyone as much as she did the ugly monster with the great moon face. Instead of answering, she coaxed Melissa toward the animals.

Melissa had been weeping and sniffling ever since Killibrew made her go behind some boulders and take off her dress. As a substitute, Killibrew had taken half of Kyle's blanket, cut a hole in the center, and instructed Melissa to slide her head through the hole and let it hang down. It was a lot like the ponchos Evelyn had seen Mexicans wear in Santa Fe.

"I want my dress, darn him," Melissa complained. "That mean man had no right to take it."

Killibrew heard her. "Quit your gripin', girl. Your pa got the point, and that's all that counts."

"My pa?" Melissa said, and lifted her head to say more.

"Don't!" Evelyn whispered.

"But they think we're sisters," Melissa replied.

"I know." Evelyn had caught on at the glade. She couldn't explain why, but she felt it was important they not reveal the truth. "Let them go on thinking it," she advised.

Bittner impatiently motioned at them. "What did we tell you about that infernal whispering? When you have something to say, say it out loud."

"We don't want you plottin' behind our backs," Killibrew said. "We'll treat you decent, but only so long as you do as we say."

Evelyn and Melissa separated. Evelyn was hauled up behind Kyle; Melissa had to ride double with Bittner.

"Better hold on tight," Kyle suggested. "I wouldn't want you to fall off and hurt yourself."

Evelyn thought it silly. From what she had seen, she was a better rider than he was.

She had her parents to thank. They had put her on a pony almost as soon as she could walk; she had many fond recollections of being led around the corral by her father or mother. When she was old enough to handle the reins herself, they had taken her for short rides. By the time she was six she could ride well enough to keep up with her older brother, and by ten years of age she was the equal of whites twice her age.

Her pa had always been of the opinion that girls should be as versed in wilderness survival as boys. He'd taught her to shoot, and how to read sign, and how to live off the land so she need never fear being lost or on her own in the woods.

Evelyn had done her best to make him proud of her. Over the past few years, though, she had lost interest in woodlore and become more involved in doing things her mother liked to do: sewing, knitting, baking, and other home skills that would come in handy when she married and had a family of her own. Her father never said anything, but she could tell he was a bit disappointed. Just as her mother was disappointed that she was more partial to white ways than those of the Shoshones.

Evelyn couldn't help it. She liked store-bought dresses more than buckskins. She liked shoes more than moccasins. She liked to sleep in a bed instead of on the ground, and she liked living in a cabin more than in a lodge. She was fond of doing her hair up, and playing with dolls, and she loved to read and draw. Her uncle Shakespeare once remarked that she was "all girl," and Evelyn took that as the highest compliment anyone ever paid her. She *was* a girl, and she enjoyed doing girl things. Was that so bad?

The pass opened before them, a defile in the rock wall. Evelyn had been through it once before, three years ago, with her father. High walls reared on either side, shutting out what little light remained, and they rode in near-complete darkness, the plod of hooves and the creak of saddles loud in the narrow confines.

Beyond the pass the towering Rockies stretched into the twilight distance for as far as the eye could see. Clear to Canada, Evelyn's father maintained. Largely unexplored except by trappers who had crisscrossed the region in the early days in search of beaver pelts, it was roamed by hostile war parties of Bloods, Piegans, and Blackfeet. The Sioux, too, occasionally drifted to its borders.

In all that vastness dwelled only two whites Evelyn knew of. Shakespeare McNair, her father's best friend and the oldest white man in the mountains, lived with his Flathead wife twenty-five miles to the north. Much closer was one other homestead: her brother's.

As Evelyn stared out across the benighted landscape, an idea took root—a bold idea that entailed considerable risk. She thought about it long and hard as her abductors meandered down the facing slope into thick firs, and decided it was worth the try. If it worked she would be free of their clutches. If not, the worst she imagined they would do was

49

beat her. They needed her alive to swap for her father's gold.

Kyle was glancing right and left, nervous at being abroad so late. Bittner and Killibrew were also high-strung. Only the half-breed, Haro, rode with the calm assurance of one at home in the wilds.

On a shelf a hundred yards lower Killibrew called a halt. It was a poor spot for a camp, in Evelyn's estimation—much too open, too exposed to the wind and the elements—but she didn't say a thing as Killibrew ordered Bittner to chop firewood, Kyle to prepare their supper, and Haro to stand guard.

Melissa was a portrait of depression. Evelyn guided her to one side and they hunkered in the high grass.

"How are you holding up?" Evelyn asked.

"How do you think? I'm scared and I'm hungry and I'm cold." Melissa plucked at the blanket. "And this itches something awful."

Evelyn leaned close to the smaller girl's ear. "I have a plan. We're going to give them the slip."

"What good would that do?" Melissa said louder than she should. "How far would we get on our own? We're in the middle of nowhere."

"My brother lives ten to twelve miles in that direction." Evelyn pointed to the northwest. "If we can reach his place—"

"Ten miles?" Melissa said, making it sound like one thousand. "Just the two of us? With no food? No water?"

"We can do it," Evelyn assured her. "I've been through this country. My pa taught me which landmarks to remember."

"What about bears? And mountain lions? And wolves?" Melissa morosely scratched herself. "I don't cotton to being eaten."

Evelyn had never met anyone so fond of always looking at the bad side of things. "Wolves don't usually attack unless they're hungry. Mountain lions will run if you yell at them. And bears aren't as fierce as everyone makes them out to be." That last was a fib. If anything, the opposite was the case. Grizzlies were rightly regarded as the scourge of the high country, and would dine on anything they could catch and kill. Including people.

The grass rustled, and Bittner loomed in the gathering gloom. "Are you two at it again? Damn. From now on, keep your mouths shut unless we say it's all right to talk."

"Yes, sir," Melissa said, cowering.

"How about you?" the bearded giant demanded of Evelyn.

"Can we breathe without permission?"

Bittner hiked a hand as if to hit her but was distracted by a grating laugh from Killibrew. "I'm glad you think this is so funny, pard."

"It's not them, it's you," the short man corrected him. "They're kids, for cryin' out loud. What can they do against the four of us? A little whisperin' ain't going to hurt none."

"Maybe. Maybe not." Bittner's hand dropped to his side. "But I don't like it. Hear me, Miss Sassy?" He was addressing Evelyn. "Any more out of you and I'll slap you silly." He tromped off to chop wood.

Evelyn bent toward Melissa. "It won't be until later, when most of them are asleep. Be ready to go when I say."

Uncertainty etched the smaller girl; her throat bobbed when she swallowed. "Can I be honest? Being out there in the dark scares me more than being with them. I really don't want to do it."

"Trust me. I won't let anything happen to you," Evelyn said. But it was a tall order. On their own and unarmed, they were prime quarry for every predator for miles around. She envisioned them running into a roving grizzly and almost changed her mind. They would stand no chance at all. It would tear them to ribbons before they could so much as scream. Her pa might track them later and give their bleached bones a burial, provided the bear left any.

"Get over here where we can keep a better eye on you," Killibrew commanded. He was beside Kyle, who was on his knees, rummaging in a pair of saddlebags.

Clasping Melissa's hand, Evelyn did as they were bid. "What are we having for supper?" she inquired. "I'm starved." She always was about mealtime. Her pa liked to joke that he could set his pocket watch by her stomach.

Kyle smiled at them. "Soup will have to do. It's too dark to go after game."

That it was. The sun was long vanquished, and a myriad of stars filled the celestial vault of inky sky. Evelyn did as her father had taught her and scoured the land below for sign of campfires. There were none. Swiveling to the north-west, she probed the woodland for a gleam of light from her brother's cabin, but the intervening forest concealed it from prying eyes. Much to her relief.

"Blame your folks," Killibrew snapped. "If they hadn't delayed us back there, we'd have made it through the pass a lot sooner and could have got some huntin' done." He stalked toward the horses.

"Pay him no mind," Kyle said. "He was born grumpy, and his disposition hasn't improved much with age."

Evelyn scrutinized the young man with renewed interest. Of all of them, he was the only one who treated them decently. The only one who shared kind words now and then. "What you're doing is wrong," she bluntly stated.

Kyle froze in the act of removing a large piece of pemmican from the saddlebags. "I wouldn't be so quick to judge, were I you. When you're older, you'll realize that sometimes we have to do things we don't want to."

"I could live to be a hundred and I'd never steal children," Evelyn said.

Kyle's cheeks pinched inward. "Killibrew has promised me you won't be harmed. He has it all worked out. All your father has to do is hand over the gold and the two of you will be set free."

"What if he's wrong? What if my pa doesn't have any gold?" Evelyn said. "Will he hang us for real?"

Kyle drew a long-handled Green River knife and slashed into the pemmican. "I was at Bent's Fort. I heard them talking about your father's nuggets."

"What if that was all he had?" Evelyn amended.

Gripping the strip he had cut off, Kyle looked her in the eyes. He was troubled, and it showed. "It won't work. Maybe if you'd swear on your mother's life you're telling the truth, I'd be inclined to believe you."

"What would that prove?"

"I didn't think you would," Kyle said smugly, and resumed slicing. "Nice try, though. You had me hoodwinked there for a second."

Evelyn squared her shoulders and said in all earnestness, "May my mother be tortured and scalped by Blackfeet if what I've told you isn't gospel." The gospel part she added because she had heard a lot of her father's friends use the expression, usually when they'd had too much to drink and someone accused them of exaggerating a tale.

Kyle froze a second time and said sternly, "Don't play games with me, girl. I won't stand for it."

"My pa isn't as rich as your friend makes him out to be, or we wouldn't be living in a cabin in the mountains," Evelyn persisted, fibbing her heart out. "We'd live in a mansion in St. Louis and I'd have all the pretty clothes I wanted." Her father visited St. Louis every other year or so, and she always tagged along. It was a whole new world, a world she reveled in. Her favorite pastime was to shop until her legs were fit to fall off. At night they sometimes attended the theater, and she couldn't get enough of the wonderful costumes and the marvelous music. To her, the glories of refined society had the dire dangers of the wilderness beat all hollow.

Kyle chopped at the pemmican as if trying to kill it. "I refuse to believe you. Do you hear me? Go away and don't bother me."

David Thompson

Out of the night strode Bittner, his arms laden with dead branches. "What's the matter, boy? Are these brats giving you a hard time?"

"No," Kyle said, but he didn't sound convincing. "And don't call me 'boy.' I'm not your son or anyone else's."

"Touchy whelp, aren't you?" Bittner said, not the least bit intimidated. Dumping the firewood at Kyle's feet, he said gruffly, "Get the fire started. I have me a hankering for some of that hot chocolate we never got to drink."

"Start the fire yourself, you lummox," Kyle said testily.

Evelyn leaped back, pulling Melissa after her, as the big man seized Kyle by the front of his shirt and jerked him erect. The next instant Kyle's knife flashed dully, and he pressed the razor tip against Bittner's hairy jugular.

"Stop that, you jackasses!" Out of the night rushed Killibrew. Shouldering between them, he shoved the two men apart. "What the hell has gotten into you lunkheads? We're in this together, remember? It won't work if we turn on each other like rabid wolves."

"This ox started it!" Kyle spat through clenched teeth.

Bittner balled fists as round as wagon-wheel hubs. "Call me that again and you'll eat your teeth."

Furious, Killibrew gave each another shove. "Listen to yourselves! You sound like a couple of brats who can't—" Blinking a few times, he fixed Evelyn and Melissa with a quizzical expression. "Why do I have the feelin' you two are responsible for this? What did you do?"

"It wasn't them," Kyle came to their defense. "Bittner just likes to throw his weight around."

"Enough!" Killibrew shook his fist under the younger man's nose. "I made it plain at the beginnin'. No fightin'. Ever. Too much is at stake. Now, get back to work!"

Bittner shrugged and ambled off for more firewood. "Whatever you say. You're the boss."

Simmering like a steam kettle, Kyle slowly knelt. He stabbed at the pemmican instead of cutting it, a storm cloud roiling on his forehead.

54

Killibrew held his rifle horizontal at his waist and advanced on Evelyn and Melissa, pushing them out of earshot of the others. He wasn't rough, but he wasn't gentle, either. Squatting, he coolly palmed his dagger and held the double-edged blade to Melissa's neck. He did it so fast, she couldn't dodge or run.

"Don't hurt her!" Evelyn pleaded.

Melissa whined like a puppy, the whites of her eyes bright in the gloom.

"Whether your sister suffers depends on whether you cause me more trouble," Killibrew said harshly. "I saw you talkin' to Kyle. I don't know what you said, but I won't stand for any more shenanigans. Am I clear?"

"We understand," Evelyn said.

"I hope so, brat, for your sakes." Killibrew shoved the dagger into its sheath and rose. "Next time I'll cut her. I need you alive, but I don't need you in one piece." Pivoting, he departed, humming to himself.

Evelyn embraced Melissa, who had started to cry, and patted her back. "You're safe now. He's gone."

"We'll never be safe," Melissa whimpered, and dug her fingers into Evelyn's shoulders. "I take back what I said. We have to escape, no matter what."

Chapter Five

Evelyn King's eyelids felt as heavy as the lumps of lead her pa melted down to make bullets. She was trying to stay awake, but it became harder with every passing minute. Again and again her eyes drooped shut and she felt herself drifting to sleep. Again and again, marshaling her energy, she snapped them open again. She couldn't hold out much longer, though. A pleasant sluggish feeling was creeping through her body, fatigue so potent it dulled her will to resist.

Based on the position of the Big Dipper, Evelyn calculated it was somewhere between two and three in the morning. Killibrew, Kyle, and Haro were asleep. Bittner was keeping watch. He had relieved Killibrew an hour ago and was now hunched over, cross-legged, near the fire. He had gulped down a cup of coffee, but it didn't have much effect. His elbows were propped on his knees and his bearded chin was propped in his hands, and every now and then he slumped toward the ground, only to straighten with a start when he realized he was dozing off.

Evelyn considered bashing him over the head with a rock but was afraid she wasn't strong enough to knock him out. Besides which, the noise might awaken the others. Mired in shadow, she peered out from under the blanket they had given her, praying Bittner would fall asleep before she did. Soon her eyelids drooped for the umpteenth time, and it took every ounce of willpower she had to open them again.

It was important they escape before dawn, not the next night or the one after. Her brother's cabin wasn't all that far. Another day or two of travel would double and triple the distance they had to cover, and double and triple the likelihood of running into hostiles or a hungry predator.

Evelyn thought of Zach and his wife, Louisa, and how much fun she'd had on her last visit. Zach had changed a lot since he got hitched. He didn't tease and torment her as he had when they were younger. He didn't call her names or tug on her hair or make those grunting sounds that used to annoy her to no end. Marriage had matured him, turned him into a whole new person.

Much to her surprise, Evelyn sort of missed the old Zach at times. She'd mentioned how different he was to her father one day, and her pa had bestowed a kindly smile and said, "It happens to everyone sooner or later. We can't stay children forever, as much as some of us would like to."

"When I was little I never wanted to grow up," Evelyn had confided. "I wanted ma and you to look out for me always."

Her father had chuckled. "That's normal. It takes courage to grow up, to stand on our own two feet. In the big cities back east, people can put it off a lot longer than they can out here on the frontier."

"How do you mean, Pa?"

Her father had encompassed their valley with a sweep of his arm. "Out here life is a lot harder. If we don't hunt, we starve. If we don't learn how to find water, we die of thirst. If we don't know how to start a fire without a flint and steel, we can freeze to death in the dead of winter. And we never know from one day to the next when someone or something will try to kill us. Either we learn to deal with life on its own terms, or life buries us. We have to deal with the reality of it all at a lot younger age than city folks."

"But they have to eat and drink and wear clothes, too," Evelyn had pointed out.

"It's not the same. In most big cities and towns a person can walk into a restaurant or a tavern at practically any hour of the day or night and get a bite to eat. The same when they're thirsty. When they need new clothes, they can walk into a store and buy it right off the rack. And they don't have to worry about hostiles or wild beasts."

"That makes them less mature?"

"In a sense, yes. Civilization shelters them. It provides the food they eat and the water they drink and the clothes on their backs. They have no need to learn to fend for themselves. So they never learn to face life as it is. And they never become fully mature."

"I still don't quite understand," Evelyn had admitted.

"Life is about learning. The older we get, the more experiences we have, the wiser we become. The more mature we become. That's the natural order of things. But in civilized society, a lot of people never become as mature as they should be because they never have the experiences they need to make them mature."

Evelyn had given their talk considerable thought. City life had always appealed to her much more than life on the frontier, and she planned to move to a city one day, much to her mother's dismay. She would have a nice house and wear pretty clothes and go to the theater and formal balls, just like the ladies in St. Louis did. Life would be so much easier and a lot less dangerous, and she saw nothing wrong in that.

Random images flitted through Evelyn's mind. She remembered the first time she had visited St. Louis and been dazzled by the glitter and the glamour. She remembered dragging her mother into every millinery they passed, and trying on dresses and hats and shoes. She remembered how glorious it was to eat hot meals without having to slave over a hot stove to prepare it.

Then Evelyn didn't think of anything for a while, and when next she opened her eyes, she was shocked to discover she had been asleep for over an hour. The fire had burned low. Fingers of flames were licking at charred branches. Killibrew was snoring as loud as a griz. Kyle had his blanket pulled up over his head. Haro was on his back on the hard ground, impervious to the chill, his arms folded across his painted chest. She glanced toward Bittner and almost whooped for joy.

The burly bear had oozed onto his side and was sound asleep.

Slowly sitting up, Evelyn twisted so she could see Melissa. Exhaustion had taken its toll, and the younger girl was sound asleep. Carefully easing out from under her blanket, Evelyn slid close enough to Melissa to nudge her shoulder. All Melissa did was smack her lips and mutter something. Evelyn nudged her again, harder, and Melissa swatted at her hand as if it were a troublesome fly.

Rising into a crouch, Evelyn took a gamble. She clamped her left hand over Melissa's mouth and shook. Instantly, Melissa's eyes snapped wide and she gaped in fear and confusion. "Don't make a sound!" Evelyn whispered in her ear. "It's time to go. Do exactly as I do and don't make any noise."

Melissa grew calm, and nodded.

Removing her hand, Evelyn straightened. None of the men had stirred. She pointed at a murky phalanx of vegetation at the west end of the shelf and tiptoed toward it. Melissa rose and followed, dragging her blanket behind her, and Evelyn quickly motioned for Melissa to set it down before the rustling woke their abductors. She bore to the left to give Bittner and the fire a wide berth when the glint of the firelight off metal brought her to a stop. Motioning for Melissa to stand still, Evelyn crept toward Bittner's rifle. They could use a gun, and while it was longer and heavier and a larger caliber than hers, she could use it if she had to.

Suddenly Bittner stopped snoring. Evelyn froze, petrified he was about to wake up. But after five or ten seconds he rolled onto his back and resumed snoring louder than ever. She took another wary step, and another, and was bending to reach down when Bittner mumbled in his sleep and his big arm shifted so it lay across the barrel.

Evelyn frowned and retreated. They would have to do without. She wouldn't risk wakening him. Keeping one eye on the bad men at all times, she cat-footed toward the edge of the trees.

Melissa was placing each foot down as if she were treading on eggs. She looked scared, very scared, and was biting her lower lip, but to her credit she didn't falter.

At the firs Evelyn glanced back at the sleeping forms, gripped Melissa's hand, and plunged into the forest. It was as dark as dark could be, an inky blackness relieved here and there by feeble patches of pale moonlight. She anxiously groped her way, moving slowly at first to avoid making noise, but once they had covered twenty or thirty yards and her eyes had adjusted, she doubled their pace.

Melissa's fingers were as tense and tight as wire. "Listen to all the animals!" she breathed in suppressed terror. "We'll be eaten alive!"

Evelyn was so accustomed to the bedlam of night sounds, she tended to take them for granted. In the distance a wolf uttered a waving howl. To the east, toward the prairie, coyotes yipped in ululating chorus. Somewhere to the west a mountain lion screeched like a woman in torment, and closer, but not so close it worried Evelyn, a roving grizzly coughed. "Most of them will leave us be," she whispered to soothe Melissa's nerves.

"Most?"

The fact was, Evelyn wasn't being entirely truthful. Grizzlies were as apt to devour a human as run from one. Cougars were largely unpredictable, but if they sensed fear they were more prone to attack than not. Wolves ordinarily left humans alone, although when they had gone long without making a kill, they went after anything and everything. Then there were lynx and bobcats. Not to mention wolverines. Although rare, they were widely dreaded. Her own mother once tangled with a wolverine that nearly did her in.

Evelyn hurried alertly on, for the moment unconcerned. Nighttime was predator time, but the wilderness was vast and the meat-eaters, while abundant, were nowhere near as plentiful as the elk, deer, and lesser creatures on which they routinely preyed.

A low branch nicked Evelyn's cheek, reminding her to keep her mind on the matter at hand. She avoided a thicket, slid over a musty log, and proceeded down an open slope toward another belt of trees.

"What's that?" Melissa asked, extending an arm.

Evelyn looked, and tingled from head to toe. To the northwest, many miles off, flickered a solitary pinpoint of light. It had to be Zach's cabin! Or so she concluded until she realized they were too far off. They had to traverse several intervening ridges before they would reach his valley.

"It's a campfire, isn't it?" Melissa said. "It could be hostiles."

"It might be friendly Indians or white men, too," Evelyn rebutted. The Shoshones regularly traveled through the area after buffalo. So did the Flatheads and the Nez Percé—although less frequently—neither of whom had ever harmed a white person and took pride in the fact.

One of the greatest shocks of Evelyn's early years had been the day her father told her about a pair of trappers jumped by a Piegan war party and brutally slain. She had been four or five or thereabouts, and until then she had assumed all people got along as well as her family did with the Shoshones. It upset her tremendously to learn there were tribes who hated whites for the color of their skin, and whites who hated Indians for the very same reason.

Hatred always puzzled Evelyn. She liked people, red and white. Liked getting to know them. Liked making new friends. To her, life was a grand adventure to be lived to the fullest, not spent nursing grudges and despising others for the mere sake of despising them.

It brought to mind Evelyn's second visit to St. Louis. She had been older, and she had noticed some things she hadn't noticed before. Such as the cold glances thrown at her brother and her when some people learned they were of mixed blood. Such as the signs in the windows of certain hotels that read "No Indians or Blacks Allowed." And how blacks and Indians were seated separate from the whites in the few restaurants that would admit them.

Prejudice, her pa called it. The worst kind of hatred. The kind that led to strife and wars. The kind that led those Piegans to butcher those trappers. The kind that led whites to shoot Indians on sight.

It was an insane world and not getting any saner.

A few more yards and trees closed over them, blotting out the feeble light. Evelyn hiked as rapidly as the conditions allowed. Once every minute or two she glanced over her shoulder for evidence of pursuit, but none materialized.

Melissa looked back, too, and said, "What will they do to us if they catch us? Beat us, maybe? Take a switch to our backsides?"

"They're not going to catch us," Evelyn vowed. Not if she could help it. With each yard they covered her confidence grew. Once the sun rose and she could see what she was doing, she would try some of the tricks her parents had taught her for throwing pursuers off the scent. Eluding Killibrew, Bittner and Kyle shouldn't be too difficult, but Haro was another matter. Killibrew had bragged that the 'breed was an excellent tracker, and Evelyn believed him.

More minutes dragged by. More wolves howled, more coyotes yipped. Evelyn was threading through a stand of slender aspens when a twig snapped loudly to their right. She stopped and crouched, pulling Melissa down beside her. Melissa's fingers constricted around her own like miniature snakes, and she heard the other's girl's breath flutter excitedly. Sensing she was about to speak, Evelyn put a hand over her mouth.

Off among the aspens something moved. That it was four-legged and about the size of a foal was obvious; whether it was a meat-eater or a plant-eater wasn't. Evelyn saw the head bob in a peculiar fashion, as deer were wont to do when testing the wind for sounds and scents, and she relaxed and removed her hand. "It's all right," she whispered.

As if to prove her wrong, the woods were pierced by the ringing shriek of a big cat. A mountain lion was hidden in dense brush just beyond the aspens. The deer promptly bolted, fleeing northward, bounding high with each leap. It had gone perhaps fifteen yards when a quicksilver form hurtled out of the brush after it. This one was low to the ground and moved with astounding speed. It overtook the deer in a twinkling and a pitiable bleat rent the night, a bleat punctuated by a throaty snarl, the thrash of limbs, and the crash of a heavy body tumbling end over end.

Melissa tried to stand and run, but Evelyn grabbed hold of her other arm and yanked her back down.

Ever vigilant, the cougar was astride its kill. Its sharp ears had caught Melissa's movement, and it swung toward them. Slanted eyes glowed dimly in a stray moonbeam, that penetrated the forest canopy.

"It's going to eat us!" Melissa cried.

A feral growl rose on the wind as the mountain lion stepped off the deer and sank low to the grass.

Facing it, Evelyn straightened. She mustn't show fear. She mustn't run. Fleeing from a painter provoked it to attack. Their only hope was to bluff their way out and hope the cat was more interested in its fresh kill than in them. "Stay close to me," she said, and slowly sidled westward.

Again Melissa attempted to run. Again Evelyn refused to let go. "Stay calm. We'll get out of this if we don't lose our heads."

The cat hadn't come any closer. Its tail was twitching and it voiced repeated low snarls, but it didn't attack. Presently the milky aspens gave way to tall spruce. Evelyn could no longer see it. The snarls ceased, but she held to a walk for another fifty yards anyway. Then she jogged for as long as her lungs held out.

Deep in the primeval woodland, beside a lightning-blasted tree, Evelyn halted to catch her breath. Melissa was wheezing loud enough to be heard in Missouri. They sagged onto the downed trunk, and Melissa was racked by a coughing fit that ended with her declaring, "I never want to go through anything like that again as long as I live!"

"It's a good thing your uncle is taking you back to North Carolina," Evelyn said. Shakespeare McNair liked to say that some people had no business living west of the Mississippi. Plainly, Melissa was one of them, if a little thing like a cougar rattled her so badly. To Evelyn the encounter was yet another in a long string, and she had already put it from her mind.

"I don't see why you stay in these god-awful mountains," Melissa husked. "I never wanted to live on the frontier, but my father and mother wouldn't listen."

"Parents do that," Evelyn said lightheartedly.

Melissa smacked the log in irritation. "I begged them not to come west. I told them I didn't want to leave my friends. That I was happy right where we were. But they said it would be a whole new life for us." She paused, and said sorrowfully, "There was nothing wrong with the life we had."

Through the trees a snowcapped peak was visible, rearing thousands of feet into the rarefied air. Evelyn compared it to her mental catalogue of landmarks but couldn't identify it.

"Now look!" Melissa's voice nearly broke, and she stifled a sob. "My parents are dead. My brother is dead. My sisters are dead. And all for what?"

"You can't blame your folks for doing what they thought was right," Evelyn mentioned.

"I can if it got them killed" was Melissa's rejoinder. "I'm all alone in the world now. My uncle is nice and all, and living with him will be fun, but it won't be the same. He's not my pa. His wife isn't my ma."

Anticipating another deluge of tears, Evelyn changed the subject. "Once we're rested, we're heading lower. By morning we'll need water, and there's bound to be a stream in the valley below."

"What will we do for food?"

"I'll rustle up something," Evelyn said. Truth to tell, though, without a gun it would be next to impossible to bring down game. Certain plants were edible, but finding them was sometimes even more of a challenge.

The next moment, catching Evelyn completely off guard, large wings beat heavily above them and a high-pitched screech assailed her ears. Instinctively, she recoiled and raised her arms to protect herself. Melissa screamed and dived flat. A few moments more the wings beat loudly, then they faded.

Evelyn glimpsed a silhouette outlined against the stars. "It was an owl!" she exclaimed. Why it had swooped so low, she couldn't say, unless it had been roosting in a nearby tree and just flown off.

"An owl?" Melissa whined, gazing in abject fright at the sky. "I thought it was an eagle."

"Eagles don't hunt at night," Evelyn said. She helped the smaller girl up and smoothed the blanket poncho. "Let's keep going," she recommended. They had a lot of ground to cover before dawn.

"I want to crawl into a hole and stay there until your folks come looking for us," Melissa said.

That would be a while, Evelyn reflected. Her father's meet-up with the kidnappers wasn't for three weeks. She grasped Melissa's hand and hiked on around the log and down the next slope. It was littered with loose stones and earth, and several times she slipped and nearly fell. Melissa trudged tiredly at her side. Below the talus were pines, and below the pines were acres of boulders and clumps of vegetation, intermixed.

Evelyn lost track of the passage of time, but it had to be hours. Her legs grew as heavy as her eyelids had been, and she walked stiffly, her sore feet protesting the uncommon treatment. She yearned to soak them in a basin of hot water and imagined that was exactly what she was doing. It seemed to help relieve some of the discomfort.

The dank scent of water brought Evelyn's head up. They were lower down than she had thought and the ground was leveling off. Cottonwoods were a stone's throw away, and as she had learned from her travels with her parents, where there were cottonwoods, often there was a waterway. She walked faster, sparking a grumble from her companion.

"What's your rush? I'm ready to keel over."

"How would you like to slake your thirst?" Evelyn asked.

Perking up, Melissa licked her dry lips and cracked a smile. "I'd give anything. Anything at all."

A stiff breeze fanned the cottonwoods and the high weeds under them. To the east a faint hint of pink framed the horizon, herald for impending dawn. Predators would soon retire to their dens, and the rising sun would lure animals that preferred its light and warmth out of their burrows and hideaways.

Parting the weeds with her left arm, Evelyn made a bee-line toward where she suspected the stream would be. She slowed when the weeds unaccountably fell away before her, and looking down, she saw they had been flattened in a four-foot-wide swath by a large animal that had passed by some time ago. The size of the trail was troubling. An elk was her first guess, but she scoured the earth in vain for hoofprints. A mountain buffalo was big enough, but it, too, had heavy hooves.

"What are you waiting for?" Melissa impatiently asked. "My throat is bone dry."

Evelyn was torn between hastening on or searching for sign. The matter was taken out of her hands when Melissa hurried on by. Too tired to argue, Evelyn overtook her and they wound through the cottonwoods until they came to a low bank bordering the most wonderful sight in the world: a gurgling stream. Its rushing waters flowed swiftly past, the lighter-shaded shallows broken by darker depths.

"At last!" Melissa cried, and would have leaped from the bank had Evelyn not snagged her wrist.

"Can you swim?"

"Not very well, no. Why?" Melissa stamped her foot like a horse eager to begin a race. "All I want is a drink."

"You were about to jump into a deep pool." Evelyn moved to their left, down the bank to a gravel bar. Dropping onto her hands and knees, she dipped her mouth into the water and greedily drank. It tasted so cold, so delicious, she wanted to gulp until she was fit to burst. But she remembered her mother warning her that to do so after going without for a long spell could cause cramps. So after several deep swallows she sat up and wiped her dripping chin with her sleeve.

Melissa was on her belly, guzzling madly, soaking her hair and the top of the blanket in the process.

"Don't overdo it," Evelyn cautioned.

The pink tinge to the eastern sky was now banded by streaks of yellow and orange. As if by a prearranged signal, the cries of the meat-eaters stilled and an eerie silence reigned. It was the quiet hour before the dawn, the hour when the world seemed to nap, catching its breath before the pulse of life pumped anew.

Evelyn nudged Melissa with the toe of a shoe. "Don't overdo it," she repeated. "You'll get sick."

Wet from forehead to chin, Melissa looked up and grinned. "I don't care. I could drink forever."

"Well, I care," Evelyn said. "I can't carry you, and we have a long way to go." They had another eight miles to travel, by her best reckoning. At the rate they were moving, they'd reach Zach's by evening.

"We're not stopping to rest?" Melissa rose onto her knees. "I need sleep. Lots and lots of sleep."

"Later." Evelyn moved onto the bank and scanned the stream for a likely spot to cross.

Melissa stood. "Didn't you hear me? I'm tuckered out. My legs hurt and my shoes are pinching my toes and I'm hungry and I—"

Evelyn held up a hand. "I feel the same. But you don't hear me complaining."

"You're older than I am!" Melissa declared. "Maybe you can go without rest and food, but I can't! Go on without me if you want."

"Killibrew knows we're missing by now," Evelyn said. "Haro will be on our trail, and *he* won't rest until we're caught."

"Please. I'm begging you. Just a little while."

Evelyn wavered. Melissa had a point about her being older. Plus, she had lived her entire life in the wilderness, and Melissa hadn't. She was used to hardship, to going without when need be. She looked at the other girl to tell her it would be all right to rest for an hour and saw Melissa was gawking at her in disbelief. Or, rather, *past* her at something in the cottonwoods. Thinking it must be Haro, Evelyn spun.

Up out of the high weeds had risen the creature responsible for the swath of trampled stems. It had many nicknames: bruin, silvertip, Lord of the Rockies, humpback, the Man-Slayer. Staring balefully at them from under its sloped brow was the most ferocious beast on the continent—an enormous grizzly.

Chapter Six

Winona King couldn't sleep. She tried. She honestly tried. Lying on her side next to her husband, she closed her eyes and sought to drift off, but she was too upset. Her mind raced faster than an arrow in flight. She couldn't stop thinking about Blue Flower and Melissa. Her beloved daughter was in peril, and it vexed her unbearably that for the time being there was nothing she could do about it.

Being powerless magnified Winona's misery a thousand-fold. She wanted to get the kidnappers in her gun's sights, wanted to blow out their wicks with well-placed shots and send them to the infernal hell her husband had told her many whites believed in. If anyone truly deserved to suffer in torment until the end of time, they did.

The cabin was quiet save for Nate's even breathing and periodic muffled sounds from the front room where Ezriah Hampton was bedded down next to their fireplace. They intended to head out at first light for Bent's Fort, and Nate had urged each of them to get as much rest as they could.

An impossible request, as far as Winona was concerned. She found herself recalling some of her fondest memories of her daughter. Of Blue Flower's first words, the Shoshone words for mother and father, and of her daughter's first awkward steps, giggling the whole while at her accomplishment. She remembered the many lazy summer evenings the family played tag and hide-and-seek, games taught them by her mate. She thought of their many journeys—to Santa Fe, to the Pacific Ocean, to St. Louis and elsewhere. But her fondest memory was of the many times Blue Flower had climbed into her lap on the rocking chair and the two of them had rocked back and forth for minutes on end, warmed by the crackling fire. At moments like those Winona had felt so loved, so very happy.

Being a mother was heartrending at times. Winona had never let on to her son, but she had been crushed when Stalking Coyote took a wife and moved north to a cabin of his own. Yes, she had known it would happen one day. Yes, it was part and parcel of raising a family. But that didn't dull the pain. It didn't diminish the loss.

In her more private moments of introspection, Winona admitted to herself that she was looking forward with great anxiety to the day the last of her offspring flew the nest. Blue Flower was all she had left. When her daughter went off into the world to make her own way, it would be the single saddest day of Winona's life. She would never tell Blue Flower that, of course. She would never be so thoughtless. But merely thinking about it made her feel as if her heart were being squeezed through one of those clothes wringers attached to the washing tubs white women used.

Now this.

Winona had always tried to protect her children without being too obsessive. When Blue Flower was small, Winona had limited her play area to the clearing around the cabin. Later, as Blue Flower blossomed into a typical girl and learned to use a rifle, Winona had given her the run of the lake and the surrounding woods, but no farther. And even then, Winona was always watchful, always diligent for signs and sounds of trouble.

Parental love was a cruel taskmaster. On the one hand, parents wanted their children to grow and mature so one day they would have families of their own; on the other hand, once the children were gone, it left a gaping wound in the parent's heart, an aching loneliness that couldn't be relieved.

Nurturing a child to adulthood was an immensely taxing yet infinitely rewarding task.

There were times when Winona secretly envied white women, particularly those who lived east of the Mississippi. They lived in settled communities and raised their families in peace and relative ease. Predators had long since been exterminated. There were no grizzlies to contend with, no panthers or wolves or rattlesnakes. There were no hostile war parties to fret about, no Blackfeet or Sioux in search of coup to count and scalps to lift.

Winona could barely imagine such a wonderful life, but she had no hankering to move. The wilderness was her home. She had been born and raised in the mountains, and one day she would die there. She had learned to accept the bad with the good, and make the best of it. And for all her fears, all her worries, she had to concede there were many delightful aspects to life in the wild, aspects denied those who lived in the States. How many of them could step out their door and see a majestic mountain three miles high? How many daily enjoyed spectacular sunsets that defied description? Or were treated to sweeping vistas of pristine forest and the gleaming diamond of an alpine lake? How many were treated to the sight of eagles soaring aloft on outstretched wings? Or the bugling of elk and the clash of antlered giants during rut?

The wilderness was a fount of incredible beauty; it was also a fount of incredible deadliness. Winona thought she had reconciled herself to the fact long ago. But she had been deceiving herself. For now that her precious daughter's life teetered on the brink of fickle fate, a bubbling cauldron of resentment boiled within her, resentment that the always-latent deadliness had struck too close to home. Literally.

Winona rolled onto her back and cupped a hand behind her head. Dejected, she gazed at the rafters bracing the ceiling and resigned herself to a night of tossing and turning.

"You can't sleep either?" Nate softly asked, and rolled over onto his own back and glanced at her. Sadness lined his features. He put a hand behind his own head and sighed. "I can't stop thinking about her."

"And Melissa," Winona said.

"And Melissa."

Winona idly toyed with the lace on her pink cotton nightgown, a gift from Nate on one of their visits east. "If we ride without stopping, we can reach the fort by eight tomorrow night. They bar the gate at sunset, but St. Vrain will open them for us."

"We'll take extra horses and ride them in relays," Nate proposed. "It will shave time off."

"What are we to do when we get there?" Winona asked. "Who are we to contact?"

"The kidnappers didn't say." Nate sighed. "All they told Ezriah was that directions would be waiting for us."

Winona's fear became a clawing fury in the pit of her stomach. "What if we don't find any? What if there is no one there to tell us where we are to deliver the gold? How will we find Blue Flower?"

Nate's callused hand covered hers, dwarfing it. "We'll cross that bridge when we come to it. If worse comes to worst, we'll ask for volunteers to help us scour the countryside."

That gave Winona an idea. "And I will ride to Touch the Clouds and ask him for the help of my people." Her cousin was a renowned leader, chief of his village, adviser and counselor to three hundred and fifty-two men, women, and children, and one of the three most influential warriors in the entire Shoshone nation. He adored Blue Flower. She was sure she could prevail on him to send riders to other Shoshone villages. Within a week, hundreds of warriors would be involved in the hunt.

They were silent a bit, each of them lost in their own thoughts. Then Nate remarked, "Ezriah still wants to go with us."

"No."

"You can't blame him for what happened. He's lucky those men didn't kill him."

Winona saw things differently. Hampton should have brought the girls back to the cabin the instant he saw the footprints by the lake. The way he told it, only a few seconds elapsed between the time he saw the tracks and when the four men appeared. But he still should have tried to get the girls out of there. She bared her sentiments to her husband.

"You're being unfair," Nate said, not unkindly. "If either of us had been there, we'd have done the same thing."

"Perhaps," Winona grudgingly agreed. But she couldn't find it in her heart to forgive him. The old trapper had been a thorn in her side since they met him. Ezriah delighted in teasing her, in always citing the thousand and one faults of womankind to stress her own. He took almost perverse delight in making her angry, and would cackle like crazy whenever he succeeded. She was constantly mad at him, but it didn't bother him one whit. Strangely enough, he thrived on her anger, and he went to considerable lengths to get her goat each and every day.

"He was outnumbered," Nate defended the oldster. "If he had gone for his guns, the girls might have been caught in the crossfire. Would you rather have had that?"

Winona refused to dignify the question with a reply.

"He's profoundly sorry the girls were taken. He's apologized dozens of times. And he'd like to make good by helping us find them. What more can he do?" Nate stared at her, awaiting an answer.

"Can I help it if I do not think as highly of him as you do?" Winona said more severely than she intended.

"Is that what this is about? He's got your dander up so many times it won't ever come down?" Nate's grin was clearly defined in the darkness. "I never thought I'd live to see the day when you would be so childish."

In all the years of their union, her husband had never once insulted her. Nate was always so considerate, so tactful, that to hear him accuse her of immature behavior left Winona temporarily speechless. For him to do it so cavalierly was salt on the verbal wound. Sitting up, she declared, "I will have you know I am proud of the fact I have not once lost my temper with him."

"I've said it before and I'll say it again. If you want him to stop badgering you, all you have to do is ignore him."

Winona's anger mounted. "And I have said it before and I will say it again. He has stayed with us long enough. It is time he got on with his life. Time he went elsewhere. *Anywhere* would do."

"He's planning to head east with Melissa's uncle," Nate said. "Another month and he'll be out of your hair for good."

The mention of Melissa rekindled Winona's misgivings for the girls. Tears welled up, and she bowed her head so her husband wouldn't see them. To her, crying was a sign of a weak character. Shoshone girls were taught from an early age to bear hardship without complaint or the chronic shedding of tears. They were to be as strong, in their way, as the warriors were in theirs. Tears were acceptable only in certain special circumstances, the loss of a loved one enthroned at the top of the shortlist.

Practical reasons existed why crying was frowned upon, foremost among them being that loud sounds carried long distances. If the wind was blowing just right, the racket raised by a wailing woman could carry for half a mile or more—right to the eager ears of an enemy war party.

Shoshone women went about their daily duties quietly and efficiently, and while they liked to laugh and sing and enjoy themselves, always at the backs of their minds was the thought that they shouldn't be too loud or the consequences could be disastrous.

"I am glad he is leaving," Winona said belatedly. "He has caused nothing but trouble."

"That's not entirely true," Nate took issue. "He always helps out with the chores, doesn't he? He chops wood. He feeds the horses. He offered to skin the bobcat you shot."

"And did a poor job of it," Winona said. So poor, she would be lucky to get half the money she normally did when she sold it at the fort.

"The important thing is he offered," Nate said.

Winona could see the debate would get them nowhere, so she delved to the meat of the issue. "I just want our lives to be as they were before this whole business began. I want to have the cabin to ourselves, and live as a family again."

"We already do."

"It is not the same," Winona disagreed. In the old days, she could run around their cabin in the heavy robe he had bought her, when she wanted, but not now. In the old days, she liked to work in the garden with her dress hiked up around her knees, but she couldn't nowadays. The only man permitted to see her in the slightest degree of undress was her husband. No one else. Ever. Period.

Nor did Winona feel comfortable being intimate with another man in the cabin. Among her people sexual relations were accepted as a matter of course, and it wasn't unusual for a man and wife to indulge their passion in a lodge full of family members. But she wasn't about to do so in the presence of strangers.

"When this is over I want him gone," Winona said. "If he goes with Melissa's uncle, fine. But one way or the other, I want him out of our lives."

Ezriah Hampton seldom enjoyed a decent night's sleep anymore. He hadn't in ages. Ever since he had reached fifty he rarely slept more than three or four hours a night, even when he was dog tired. Someone once told him that the older a person was, the less sleep they needed, and evidently it was true.

Flat on his back on the bearskin rug in front of the King fireplace, a blanket tucked to his chin, he listened to the conversation in the bedroom and winced at each of Winona's biting comments. As was always the case when he was upset, his good eye started to jiggle like a bug on a hot rock.

Ezriah hadn't realized that Winona thought so poorly of him. Once again his mouth had gotten the better of him and offended someone he cared about and wouldn't want to hurt in a million years.

It had always been that way.

At the tender age of seven a cousin had punched him in the mouth after he made a less-than-flattering comparison between the cousin's face and the rear quarters of the cousin's dog. At ten he had been slapped by a girl who didn't appreciate having her mouth compared to a dead worm. At fourteen he had been involved in a fight with two older boys behind the general store where he'd worked in Baltimore after he remarked it must tax their mental capacity to open and close doors. When he was nineteen he had been involved in a tavern brawl after he accused a bartender of watering down the liquor.

Those were just the highlights. Year in and year out, Ezriah's mouth had landed him in more hot water than most ten men. It fueled his cynical outlook on life, an outlook that stemmed from the death of his father on his sixth birthday. His father had been hurrying home with a present for his birthday and been struck and crushed by an out-of-control freight wagon.

A fluke, everyone called it. Just one of thousands of fatal accidents that occurred every year. But those accidents happened to *other* people, and Ezriah never forgave the Almighty for depriving him of the one person who loved him selflessly and completely. His mother, while having her tender moments, couldn't be bothered to devote much attention to him. A son, interestingly enough, she'd never wanted. A son who, she never tired of pointing out, was an "accident" in himself.

It didn't help that Ezriah had been born with a rapier wit. Glib remarks—some called them insults—rolled off his tongue in a nonstop torrent. Ironically, not everyone admired his sense of humor. More often than not, the recipients of his wit took extreme umbrage and sought to do him bodily harm.

Ezriah wearied of their stupidity, wearied of those to whom hypocrisy was a way of life and lies were voiced as gospel. He had moved into a small shack on the outskirts of Baltimore and was perfectly content keeping his own company.

Then a chance run-in with a trapper fresh in from the mountains of the far West changed everything. The trapper waxed eloquent about the grand adventure of frontier life. About the fantastic sights few men had ever seen. About the thrill of venturing where only a handful of brave souls had gone before. But what interested Ezriah most were the trapper's offhanded remarks about the immensity of the wide-open spaces. How a man could travel for weeks on end and not meet another living soul. How a trapper's life was a solitary life, "the loneliest profession in the whole wide world."

78

A week later Ezriah sold most of his personal belongings to raise a stake, and mounted on a swayback nag, he'd headed west. In St. Louis he had stocked up on provisions and bought two packhorses. He'd also been embroiled in a donnybrook at a local liquor mill after he indelicately made mention of the resemblance between a foulmouthed barmaid and the sounds his lower orifice produced after a plate of baked beans.

It was early May when Ezriah started across the prairie. Deer and elk were so plentiful, his only problem was deciding which to shoot for supper. Buffalo were everywhere. It took three weeks to reach the Rockies, and to this day Ezriah never forgot the sheer overwhelming awe. They were everything he had been told, and more.

Up into the mountains Ezriah went, meandering ever higher until he reached what he deemed to be prime beaver country. Relying on a copy of *The Trapper's Guide* by Sewell Newhouse, who claimed trappers could make a thousand dollars a year if they heeded his advice, he went about setting up his camp and the next day placed his very first trap, manufactured, coincidentally enough, by the same Sewell Newhouse. It didn't occur to him until much later that Newhouse might have had a vested interest in publishing a manual that urged young Lionhearts into the depths of the wilds to use Newhouse's traps.

The guide did contain a wealth of valuable information, though. Ezriah relied on it in selecting his supplies, including half a dozen of Newhouse's patented steel traps, and he found that most everything the manual listed came in handy.

For over a month all went well. Ezriah had been happier than he'd ever been. Up one stream and down another he roamed, and it was a rare morning he didn't find at least one beaver waiting to be skinned.

One day, en route to check his traps, Ezriah spied smoke in the distance. He'd investigated, and lo and behold, it was a party of six trappers. They were right friendly, and astounded when they learned he was trapping by his lonesome.

"Always have a partner," cautioned one. "A man alone is easy pickings for savages and beasts alike."

Ezriah scoffed at their timidity. He hadn't seen any sign of Indians, and as for wild beasts, the most fierce animal he'd met was a jay that sometimes followed him on his daily rounds and squawked up a storm.

The trappers had asked Ezriah if he was attending the annual rendezvous, which was being held at Bear Lake that year. "Women, liquor, and frolics!" one exclaimed. "What more can you ask for?"

Intrigued, Ezriah had jotted down directions on how to reach the lake. And so it was that on a bright, sunny morning in early July he reached the south end of Bear Lake to find that the life of a trapper wasn't as solitary as he'd been led to think. Upward of a hundred trappers were on hand, as well as hundreds of Shoshones, Flatheads, and Nez Percé eager to barter for trade goods available nowhere else.

Ezriah sold the plews he had collected for the princely sum of two hundred and eighty-four dollars and fifty cents. His pockets bulging, he had strolled among the booths, and soon discovered he wasn't as rich as he thought he was. He needed to replenish his provisions, but he balked at the exorbitant prices the dealers were demanding. Everything was three to five times as costly as it had been in St. Louis. Gunpowder was going for a dollar-fifty a pound. Shot, the same. Sugar was a dollar a pound, tobacco a whopping three dollars a pound, and new traps cost nine dollars. Outright robbery, all legal and proper.

Greatly disillusioned, Ezriah had loaded his packhorses and set out for new trapping grounds. He needed to raise plews, lots and lots of plews, and to that end, he'd reckoned on locating virgin streams undefiled by human contact. To

do so entailed pushing deeper into the mountains than anyone ever had.

They say ignorance is bliss, and in Ezriah's ignorance he
blissfully penetrated into the dark heart of the wilderness.
He was the first to set foot in a valley where beaver were as
abundant as grass. Envisioning enough money to choke a
horse, he'd set out his traps and turned in that night as
cheerful as a glutton at a pig roast.

His joy was short-lived.

The next day, as Ezriah rested in camp at noon after skin-
ning four prime beaver, he'd heard rustling in the woods
and turned just as Sa-gah-lee warriors poured out of the
trees. They were on him before he could fire. In fierce triumph they bore him to the mesa on which they lived, and
for the better part of the next two decades he was held
captive.

The Sa-gah-lee were throwbacks to an earlier time, a
primitive people who had isolated themselves from the rest
of the world. They gave him the run of their sanctuary, but
he wasn't allowed to leave for fear he would return with
more of his kind.

Repeatedly, Ezriah attempted to escape. He resorted to
every trick he could think of to outwit them. Failure after
failure weighed heavily on his spirit, and after about ten
years he gave up trying. Monotonous days of boredom and
drudgery blended one into the other, and then one morning
new captives were brought in, Winona and Evelyn King,
and Winona rekindled the flame of defiance he had thought
long since extinguished. She was magnificent. She wouldn't
be cowed, wouldn't meekly accept the dictates of the *Sa-
gah-lee.* With her help, augmented by the timely arrival of
her husband, Ezriah achieved the impossible. He regained
his cherished freedom.

Ezriah owed her a debt he could never repay. He had
never told her, but he admired her immensely. Out of habit
he had taken to teasing her a lot. He did that with people

he cared for. Poking fun was his way of showing he liked someone. He never expected her to take exception. He never figured she would despise him.

Stung to his core, Ezriah eased out from under his blankets and rose. He always slept fully dressed except for his hat and cloak, so it was a small matter to gather his effects and his rifle and slink to the door without being detected. Thankfully, the bolt didn't grate when he slid it aside. Nor did the leather hinges creak when he cracked the door wide enough to slip on out.

Dawn was imminent. The eastern sky was several shades lighter than the west, and birds were warbling amid the trees.

Most of the horses were dozing. Ezriah opened the gate and entered the corral, speaking softly lest they become skittish. They hardly gave him a second glance. From the tack shed at the rear he chose a saddle blanket and saddle and threw them on the chestnut dun he had ridden the day before. He walked the horse out, slid the log rails into place, and forked leather as a golden ring banded the world.

Ezriah crossed the clearing to the trail head and paused. Gazing at the cabin door, he solemnly declared, "I owe you, Mrs. King. You saved my bacon, and I've repaid you by letting those bastards steal your pup. Well, never let it be said I don't settle my debts."

A lash of the reins, and Ezriah trotted to the lake and bore along the north shore to the glade in the woods. In his parfleche was enough pemmican to last a couple of weeks. He should be able to catch up to the kidnappers in a few days at the most. He might need to ride the chestnut into the ground, but the sacrifice of a horse to save two young lives was justifiable, in his estimation.

The trail was still as plain as the nose on Ezriah's face.

Sunlight spread across the valley, dispelling lingering tendrils of night. A doe on its way to the lake for its morning drink darted from his path. A chipmunk emerging to greet the new day scolded him for scaring it witless.

Ezriah cradled his rifle in the crook of his left elbow and imagined how happy Winona would be when he returned with Evelyn and Melissa. He hadn't forgotten the effigy. He remembered Killibrew's warning all too well. But that didn't deter him. He had something to prove—to himself and to Winona King.

Come what may.

Nate King was up before his wife. She had fallen asleep half an hour before sunrise, and he let her catch a few more winks. Dressing, he walked to the front door and was surprised to see that the bolt had been thrown. Glancing toward the fireplace, he was equally surprised that Ezriah Hampton was already up and about.

At that altitude the mornings were always brisk. Cold air bit into Nate's lungs as he strode to the corral. As he always did, he counted the horses to make sure that none had been stolen. The Blackfeet, inveterate horse thieves, had raided him several times over the years.

Nate finished the count, then counted again to be sure he wasn't mistaken. One of the animals was missing, the chestnut he ordinarily let Ezriah use. A line of hoofprints, ringed by the dew its hooves had displaced, angled to the trail down to the lake.

"What in the world?" Nate blurted, and ran to the trail head. Hampton was nowhere in sight. Perplexed, he scratched his chin and speculated aloud, "Where does that old coon think he's going?" Unbidden, his talk with Winona flashed through his mind, and an awful premonition seized him.

"Dear God! No!" Whirling, Nate flew toward the cabin as if demons were nipping at his heels.

Chapter Seven

"When you see a grizzly, don't panic. Wait and see if it runs or if it comes toward you. If you're on horseback, ride like the wind before the bear can get too close. If you're on foot, and the bear is close by, whatever you do, don't run. Running from meat-eaters goads them into running after you. The best thing to do is stand still and look them right in the eyes. Show them you have no fear. Nine times out of ten they'll back down and leave you alone."

Her father's advice filtered through Evelyn King's mind as she stared into the dark eyes of the mightiest predator in the mountains. Its bestial gaze bored into her as if seeing right through her. Its immense head, its huge hump, those legs as large as tree trunks tipped by long front claws that gleamed yellowish in the rising dawn light, were enough to send goose bumps rippling down her spine.

Sensing movement on her right, Evelyn shifted just as Melissa Braddock went to bolt. Grabbing Melissa's wrist, Evelyn whispered, "Don't move a muscle! Stand still or it might attack!"

Terrified, Melissa sought to break loose and flee, only to freeze at a rumbling growl from the monster in the cottonwoods.

The grizzly advanced a ponderous step.

Evelyn resisted an urge to do as Melissa had done, and locked eyes with the fearsome giant again. The silvertip halted. Raising its nostrils into the wind, it sniffed loudly a few times. The wind, though, was blowing from the west and carried their scent eastward, away from the bear.

Evelyn's father had once referred to grizzlies as "walking noses." She'd giggled, and he had gone on to explain that grizzlies depended on their sense of smell much more than their other senses. As with dogs and coyotes and wolves, bears identified other creatures primarily by scent. So sensitive were their nostrils, her father had seen grizzlies sniff out marmots deep in a burrow, dig them out, and devour them.

Evelyn remembered a trapper at a rendezvous whose name eluded her. He'd had a run-in with a grizzly, and was telling everyone who would listen how the bear had charged up to him snarling and baring its teeth, but stopped dead when the man stood his ground: "A single sniff and that mangy bear turned tail and fled like a bat out of Hades, girl. And do you know why? I'll tell you. The Almighty, in His infinite wisdom, has put a fear of man-smell in all His critters. That's why I haven't taken a bath in pretty near fourteen years. The more I stink, the safer I am."

Evelyn, on the other hand, took a bath once a day whether she needed it or not. She liked baths, liked to lie back in hot water and soak until her fingertips were wrinkled. Her mother was fond of them, too. They were always clean but they didn't have much of a smell about them, and Evelyn reasoned that was why the bear in front of her was confused. It couldn't decide if it wanted to dine on them.

Melissa had stopped attempting to tear loose and was rooted with fright. Her face was as pale as a bedsheet. Her lips were moving but no sounds came out, which was just as well. Any loud sound might also trigger an assault.

The grizzly growled again and took another ponderous stride. It was now only twelve feet away, its bulk blotting out the cottonwoods and looming gigantic in the predawn light. Evelyn swore she could feel its hot breath fan her cheeks. For long, tense moments she continued to meet its level gaze, even when the monster opened its gaping maw and its tapered teeth glinted in menace. For a few harrowing seconds Evelyn thought it was going to charge and rend her limb from limb.

Melissa picked that instant to mew like a kitten.

The grizzly grunted and swiveled toward her. It sniffed a few more times, then wheeled and gamboled off into the high weeds, plowing through them like a great ship plowing through the ocean. In its wake was a flattened path over a yard wide. Like a killer whale vanishing into morning fog, the Lord of the Rockies melted into the trees.

Evelyn exhaled and shuffled to a flat boulder to sit down. Her heart was hammering, her legs felt weak. Melissa plunked down beside her and the two of them stared at the spot where the grizzly had vanished, half afraid it would change its mind.

"I was so scared I almost wet myself," Melissa broke the nerve-racking silence. "I never want to go through anything like that ever again."

"That makes two of us," Evelyn said. The incident was yet another reason to move back east; being eaten alive didn't much appeal to her. They had been lucky, oh so lucky. Anything could have set the bear off. She remembered her pa mentioning once that some whites believed everyone had a guardian angel who looked out for them in times of trouble. If so, she owed her guardian a bushelful of thanks.

"How did you stare him down like that?" Melissa marveled. "He was so big, he could have smashed us both with a swat of his paw."

"I did what I had to," Evelyn said. The law of tooth and claw, her pa called it. A person did what was necessary to survive, or they died. It was that simple.

"What now?"

Evelyn rose and found her legs were working again. "Are you still tired?"

Melissa looked down at herself in wonderment. "No. Not at all. I'm wide awake. Is it because my heart was racing so fast?"

"That will do it." Evelyn should know. She'd had more than her share of hair-raising run-ins. But her main concern now was eluding their abductors. "Let's keep going," she proposed, and suiting action to words, she rose and forded the stream in the shallows adjacent to the gravel bar. The water only rose midway to her knees, but it was bitterly cold, so much so that her teeth were chattering when she reached the opposite bank. Clambering out, she stamped her legs to restore feeling to them.

Melissa crossed slowly, her hands outstretched, her fingers splayed, moving each leg a few inches at a time.

"The longer you take, the colder you'll be," Evelyn said.

"I can't help it. I'm afraid of falling in." Melissa's right foot slipped, and she stiffened. "I can't swim."

"Take your time, then. You'll be fine." To encourage her, Evelyn slid as low on the bank as she could go without falling in, then extended her arm as far as she could reach. "Grab hold and I'll pull you out."

A turtle could have beat Melissa across. After each tiny step she paused to run a foot over the rocks in front of her to satisfy herself they wouldn't slide out from under her. Another step, and their fingers entwined.

"Take it slow," Evelyn said. But not *too* slow; they had already wasted too much time. Evelyn yanked, and Melissa floundered toward her, whimpering like a puppy. Only a few inches from shore, Melissa lost her balance and pitched forward. Evelyn flung out her other arm, caught hold, and dragged the petrified girl up beside her.

"That was mean!" Melissa protested.

"I didn't do it on purpose."

Verdant forest was steps away. Evelyn moved toward it, then thought to twist and scan the slopes they had descended during their night-long trek. She saw no one. Smiling, she went to brush a limb aside when a pair of stick figures appeared, crossing a clearing a quarter of a mile above. Moving rapidly into some pines, they were lost to sight. Even at that distance the lead figure's red torso and the second man's burly build left no doubt who they were.

Evelyn ran. Melissa overtook her and demanded to know why they were pushing themselves so hard. "Because we need to," Evelyn said, and let it go at that.

Given her druthers, Evelyn would rather have stuck to the stream to throw Haro and Bittner off the trail. But the water was too deep in spots for Melissa to wade, and much too cold, even at that time of the year, for either of them to endure for any length of time.

A different ruse was called for.

Evelyn considered using a leafy branch to erase their tracks, but it wouldn't fool a seasoned tracker like Haro. The marks the branch made were just as obvious as the footprints the branch erased. No, she had to come up with something else, something that would deceive the wily 'breed and at the very least slow him down. A tall order, but she had a few ideas.

In forty yards they came to a clearing. Evelyn ran straight across it, then abruptly called out, "Stop!" and came to a halt. "Don't move!"

"What's wrong?" Melissa asked, nervously glancing at the surrounding vegetation. "What did you see?"

"I want you to do as I do." Looking behind her, Evelyn backed across the clearing, stepping in the exact same spots she had stepped before, recognizable by flattened blades of grass.

Confused, Melissa nevertheless obeyed, and when they were again under the trees, she asked, "What good did that do?"

"Time will tell." Evelyn veered to the left, skirted the clearing, then bore due west instead of to the northwest as they had been doing. If Haro and Bittner came on quickly, and if they didn't examine the prints in the clearing carefully, they'd be well past it before they realized the trail had gone cold. They'd need to backtrack, and that would take time.

Evelyn ran steadily, her shoes slapping the earth in cadence, and breathed shallow to lesson the strain. Melissa was puffing like an overworked ox, her poncho flapping with every stride.

The sun rose into full view. Golden light obliterated the last of the night, and birds and small animals filled the woodland with their songs and cries. Jays squawked shrilly. Ravens cawed while in flight. A squirrel chittered in indignation as the girls ran under the tree it was in.

An ache formed in Evelyn's side, but she ignored it. She also ignored the rumbling of her stomach. She was hungry enough to eat an elk, or a good chunk of one, and would gladly have rigged a deadfall or snare to catch game, but any delay, however brief, heightened the risk of being recaptured.

"I can't go on any more," Melissa announced after a bit. "My feet are ready to fall off."

"We can't stop yet," Evelyn belabored the obvious. Someway, somehow, they had to shake the 'breed off for good. Rocky ground would help, but there wasn't any. The soil was soft and plainly bore their prints, their heels most noticeable since the edges dug into the earth with each step. Shoes were like that. Moccasins had no heel and were less—

Their shoes! Evelyn suddenly stopped and plopped straight down. Hurriedly, she tore at the buckles to strip her left shoe off.

Melissa came to a halt and turned, a hand pressed to her side. Gasping for breath, she rasped, "What are you up to now?"

"Take off your shoes."

"Are you crazy? I can't run in my stocking feet. There are too many stones and sticks. It will hurt."

Evelyn was tired of the younger girl arguing all the time, but she patiently explained, "The only chance we have is to make it hard for them to track us. We'll carry our shoes so we don't leave any prints, and put them on only when we have to." She switched to her right shoe and pried at the strap. "Don't stand there like a dead tree. Take them off."

"It will hurt," Melissa complained, but she sat down and began removing her ankle-high footwear. "Are you hungry? I know I am."

"Don't think about food and it won't bother you as much," Evelyn said. Which was a lot easier said than done. She envisioned a heaping plate of her mother's delicious pancakes, smothered in thick butter and syrup the way she liked them. Or a bowl of oatmeal, a rare treat, layered with sugar, an even rarer treat.

Rising with a shoe in each hand, Evelyn walked westward, placing her feet down lightly on the carpet of pine needles. She left no tracks that she could see. "This just might work," she commented.

Melissa took a few tentative steps. "It's not as bad as I thought it would be," she said. "But the needles are poking me."

"You'll live." Evelyn hastened on before the other girl griped again. As much as she could, she avoided areas where there were a lot of downed branches, and rocky areas where sharp stones might claw at their feet. The sun beat down on their backs, growing warmer the higher it rose, and by midmorning they were three miles from where they had seen the grizzly.

Fatigue seeped into Evelyn's limbs. She plodded dully along, her head constantly drooping. The burst of energy she had received when the grizzly confronted them had long since evaporated. Her tiredness, combined with their lack of sleep, made Evelyn afraid she wouldn't last much longer.

Melissa was in worse shape. She walked stiffly, plodding like a starved buffalo calf on its last legs. Again and again her eyes closed and she slowed to a crawl, only to snap them open and plod gamely on at a word from Evelyn.

It reached the point where Evelyn knew they had to stop or one or both of them would collapse. She scoured the forest for an ideal place to rest up, somewhere safe from the prying eyes of men and the inquisitive noses of wild beasts. The terrain around them consisted of spruce interspersed with boulders and offered few hiding places. Then, ahead and to their right, a bluff reared, a sheer cliff sliced from a low hill. To one side, winding to the crest, was a steep, clearly defined game trail.

Evelyn bent her feet toward it. From the top she could spot their pursuers coming from a long way off. The climb, however, tested her endurance to its limit. Already on the brink of exhaustion, she had to reach deep inside of her for the strength it took to reach the crest.

Melissa was at the end of her rope. Three-quarters of the way up she sank onto her knees and declared, "Go on without me. I can't take another step. Honest."

"We're in this together," Evelyn said. Slipping an arm under Melissa's, she levered the smaller girl to her feet. Inadvertently, they stumbled and nearly pitched over the edge. Melissa, aghast, clutched Evelyn, making matters worse, and for anxious heartbeats they precariously teetered thirty feet above jagged rocks. Only by throwing them to the right onto their elbows did Evelyn prevent them from going over.

Melissa broke into tears. Tears of fury, not of fear. "I hate this!" she exclaimed. "Hate it! Hate it! Hate it! I wish those awful men had never shown up! I wish we were back at your cabin, and I could lie down and sleep for a week!"

"You'll rest soon enough," Evelyn said.

Standing up had never been so hard. They assisted each other, each too weak to do it alone. Arms draped over the other's shoulder, they trudged upward until at long last they gained the summit. The top of the bluff was relatively flat, half an acre square, and pitted with erosion-worn depressions sprinkled with sparse grass. It was in one of these, well back from the rim, that Evelyn instructed Melissa to lie down and get some sleep. Hardly had Melissa closed her eyes when she was out to the world.

Evelyn's body railed at her to follow suit, but first she tramped to the rim, shielded her eyes from the bright glare of the sun, and studied their back trail until her eyes watered and her head throbbed. Haro and Bittner weren't anywhere to be seen.

Stepping back a few yards, Evelyn sat down. She tried to stay awake a little while yet, but her body refused to be denied. A strange numbing sensation crawled up her chest and spread across her face to her hairline. She closed her eyes, and it was as if someone had extinguished a candle.

Blackness swallowed her whole.

Ezriah Hampton reached the pass at the north end of the valley shortly before noon. Dismounting, he ground-hitched the chestnut and helped himself to a piece of pemmican. The tangy, berry-flavored taste made his mouth water. Since he had so few teeth, he mainly gummed his food rather than chewed it, and pemmican, like jerky, took forever to eat.

Straddling a rocky spur, Ezriah gazed down the mountain at the slopes he had negotiated and was astounded he hadn't busted his fool neck. "You'll never learn, will you," he castigated himself for his bout of conscience. "What are these girls to you that you're risking your hide to save them?" They weren't family. They weren't blood kin of any kind. He wasn't responsible for them in any respect, yet here he was, making a damned jackass of himself just to prove to the Kings he wasn't the heartless rogue Winona had painted him. "You're getting soft in the head," he said.

The kidnappers, Ezriah calculated, were six to seven hours ahead. Since they thought they had scared the Kings off, they were bound to stop for the night. If he stuck to their trail with the persistence of a coyote after a rabbit, he should overtake them by late in the day.

Ezriah patted his rifle and pistols, each in turn. "The four of us will make buzzard bait of those scalawags," he vowed. Chomping into the pemmican, he gummed lustily. He had to admit that the prospect of tangling with them filled him with a degree of zest he hadn't experienced in a good long while. "Imagine that. A man my age," he said, and laughed at his folly.

Far below, something moved. Ezriah looked closer, and swore. "Hellfire. I didn't ask them to dog my heels! They should be on their way to Bent's Fort by now."

The two riders were so far off that their features were a blur, but they could only be Nate and Winona King. "Don't they care about their seedling?" Ezriah muttered. "They'll ruin everything if they aren't careful."

Ezriah had half a mind to push some boulders down on them to drive them off, but there weren't any boulders handy. Standing, he stepped to the sorrel and slid his foot into the stirrup. He had an hour's lead, maybe less. With the Kings after him, he couldn't stop again until he caught up with Killibrew and company.

On he rode.

The pass was ablaze with sunlight. Ezriah whistled to himself as he trotted through to the other side, and once in the open made no effort to hide. Why should he, when the kidnappers were half a day ahead? He had barely begun his descent when the charred remains of a campfire drew him to a shelf where the vermin had spent the night.

Ezriah circled the shelf on horseback to determine which direction Killibrew had taken and was mystified to learn that the quartet had split up. Two of the hardcases had gone off to the northwest on foot. Since one wore moccasins, it had to be Haro. The second man's tracks were as large as a bear's. That had to be Bittner.

The others had ridden north.

"This makes no kind of sense," Ezriah told the chestnut. It stood to reason that Killibrew had taken the girls with him, so with a nudge Ezriah sent the chestnut down the next slope after the four horses.

Unease gnawed at him, a vague feeling something wasn't quite right, but Ezriah shrugged it off. Wherever Haro and Bittner were bound, he fully expected them to link up with Killibrew and Kyle later on. It was essential he catch up before then. By splitting up, the kidnappers had unwittingly played into his hands and cut the odds by half. Now there were only two to deal with.

Ezriah hoped Winona appreciated the trouble he was going to in order to prove he wasn't the cad she'd branded him. Once he rescued Evelyn and Melissa, an apology was in order.

Ezriah loved it when he made others eat crow.

"I will stake him out on the ridge at the west end of our valley," Winona declared. "I will pour honey over him to attract bears. Or maybe I will kill a deer and cover him with its blood to lure in a mountain lion."

Nate King's mouth was buttoned shut. He wasn't ignoring his wife, exactly. He was letting her vent her feelings without interruption so she would be less inclined to put a hole in the old trapper's skull the moment she laid eyes on him. Or so he hoped.

Nate had rarely seen Winona so mad as she was when he burst into their cabin and informed her that Hampton had gone after the girls alone. She wasn't violent by nature, but he shuddered to think what she would have done if she had gotten her hands on Ezriah earlier.

"His recklessness endangers our daughter," Winona fumed. "What would make him do such a thing?"

"He probably thinks he's doing us a favor," Nate said. A simple enough reply, yet he had lit the fuse to a powder keg.

"A favor?" Winona exploded. "He might as well throw Evelyn and Melissa off a cliff! The result would be the same!" She mumbled in Shoshone, something about a knife and private parts. "This Killibrew, he will assume we put Hampton up to it, and will punish the girls."

Nate shared her fear, but admitting it would make matters worse. "We don't know that for sure," he hedged to calm her.

"I know I will hunt them to the ends of the earth if they harm one hair on Blue Flower's head," Winona pledged.

Further conversation was nipped by their arrival at the steep slope below the tree where the kidnappers had hung the lifelike effigy wearing Melissa's dress. Dismounting, they climbed on foot, the reins wrapped around their wrists. The bay and the mare were as surefooted as any horse on the frontier, but talus necessitated a slow pace.

They had passed the tree and were ascending the hardest slope yet when Winona coughed to clear her throat of the dust they were raising. "Do you want to know what bothers me the most, husband?"

Nate thought he knew. "Our valley was invaded. Our haven from the rest of the world isn't as safe as we'd like it to be. More and more whites are coming to the mountains, and fewer and fewer are men of moral fiber like Scott Kendall and Simon Ward. The new batch are outcasts and outlaws who prey on decent settlers like wolves on sheep.

You're afraid this won't be the last time something like this happens, and I don't blame you."

"No. That is not it."

So much for reading his spouse's mind, Nate reflected. "Then what?"

"Blue Flower plans to leave us when she is old enough. Time and again she has told us the mountains are no fit place for a family to live. Time and again I have tried to get her to see that the freedom we enjoy is worth the risks we entail. Now these evil men have come along and proven her right, and she will be more determined than ever to go off on her own."

They had debated the issue countless times, and Nate no longer took part when his wife and daughter locked horns. He sympathized with Winona's desire to have Evelyn live nearby, as Zach was doing, but he also empathized with his daughter's yearning to live where her life wasn't in danger every time she stepped out the door.

"My mother warned me this might happen," Winona said.

Nate glanced back. Morning Dew had been slain by Blackfeet not long after they met, decades ago, and not once in all that time had Winona ever mentioned her mother's outlook on their marriage. "What would?"

"She said mixed marriages are both good and bad medicine, or, as you whites would say, a blessing and a curse." As always, Winona's grasp of English was excellent. She was a much better linguist than he was. "The blessing is that the children are the product of two cultures and are that much wiser for it. The curse is that sometimes the children choose one culture over the other, and one parent suffers as a consequence."

"Your mother said all that?"

"And more. Do not misconstrue, husband. She liked you. She said you were pure of spirit. But in her heart she was sad I did not take a Shoshone warrior as my mate."

"Oh." Nate felt as if someone had lanced his side with a spear.

"Why the long face? I married you, did I not? Never once have I regretted it." Winona smirked. "Although you can be aggravating, as all men are, and more stubborn than most."

Nate laughed, pleased she was no longer boiling with rage. His gaze happened to fall on her left hand, on the first two fingers, the same fingers she had mutilated when her parents were slain. As was Shoshone custom, she had chopped the tips off. Funny how he hadn't thought about that in years.

"The men we are after do not know it yet, husband, but they are dead men. For the terrible deed they have done, for the anguish in my heart now and the anguish I will suffer if Blue Flower goes east, they will not leave these mountains alive."

Funny, too, Nate thought, how he tended to forget how fierce his wife could be.

Chapter Eight

The sensation of heat on Evelyn King's face woke her up. Her eyes opened and she went to sit up, but her body refused to respond. She felt bloated, like a deer intestine that had lain too long in the sun, and sluggish as a snail. Not to mention how sore her legs and feet were. So she lay quietly, gathering her energy, and listened to Melissa snore lightly close by.

The sun was on its westward descent. Evelyn had slept most of the afternoon away. She hadn't wanted to, but as exhausted as she had been, it was a wonder she hadn't slept longer. Rising on her elbows required a tremendous effort. Other than a hawk circling lazily to the south, the wilderness was still, the woodland serene.

Evelyn sat up, twisted her head to relieve a cramp in her neck, then stiffly rose. Her legs complained at being put to work, but she grit her teeth and shuffled to the edge of the bluff for a look-see. Nothing stirred below or in the nearby forest. She looked left, along their back trail, and suddenly her fatigue and sore muscles were forgotten and she flattened on her belly with only her eyes and forehead above the rim.

Two figures were several hundred yards off, the foremost bent low to the ground, studying it intently. Dappled by shadow, they were no more than shadows themselves.

Evelyn knew who it was: Haro and Bittner. The half-breed was doing the tracking, and he was right on their trail. It was slow going, though. As small and lightweight as she and Melissa were, in their stockings the only sign they left were smudges and scrapes. Enough for an exceptional tracker to follow, sure, but only very slowly. Each strip of soil had to be examined for the tiniest of marks. Evelyn had helped her pa track small game on many occasions and knew how difficult it could be.

Sliding back from the edge, Evelyn rose and bent over her companion. "Melissa?" she whispered. "Time to wake up."

The young girl snored on.

Evelyn gently shook Melissa's shoulder, but all Melissa did was roll onto her side. Shaking harder, Evelyn said forcefully, "Wake up, darn it! We have to get out of here."

Melissa groaned, blinked a few times, and mumbled, "What's all the fuss about? Leave me be. I want to sleep."

"You can't," Evelyn said, and tugged. "They're still after us. On your feet! Now!"

"Ah, jeez. I was having such a great dream." Melissa slowly sat up and yawned. "I feel as if I was stomped by a mule and left for dead."

"Get up." Moving behind her, Evelyn boosted Melissa upright. "We'll head off over the next rise. If we can stay ahead of them until dark, we'll be safe until morning. Haro can't track at night." Not even Apaches could and they were the best trackers alive.

Melissa took a few awkward steps, shambling stiffly as Evelyn had done. "My legs don't want to move."

"Keep at it. They'll limber up." Evelyn stepped to the north end of the bluff. There, a grassy slope rose to a forested tableland. Once they were in among the trees they would be invisible to their pursuers, but getting there across that open slope was daunting. All Haro or Bittner had to do was look up, and Melissa and she would stand out like white mountain sheep on a mountain peak.

"I'm awful hungry," Melissa mentioned.

"Not now." Evelyn dropped onto her hands and knees, her shoes in her hands. "We'll crawl to the top. Stay low." She went first, casting a look over her shoulder at the figures in the woods. The 'breed and the big man were passing through some spruce, and at the moment Haro was hunkered down, seeking sign. She faced forward, pumped her legs and arms, and didn't look back again until she reached the top. Lying on her belly, she rotated.

Melissa was only halfway up. She had little enthusiasm for the climb and was taking her sweet time.

Evelyn beckoned to spur Melissa to move faster, but the younger girl maintained the same plodding pace.

Haro and Bittner were on the move again, coming straight toward the bluff. In another couple of minutes they would be in the open, and they couldn't fail to spot Melissa.

"Hurry!" Evelyn whispered.

"I'm coming, I'm coming," Melissa replied, but she made no attempt to increase her speed.

Next to Evelyn's leg was a rock the size of a walnut. Hefting it, Evelyn held it so Melissa could see. "I'll count to ten. If you're not up here by then, I'm throwing this at you."

"You wouldn't."

"One."

Melissa grinned as if it were a huge joke.

"Two."

"What has gotten into you? I'm doing the best I can."

"Three."

Anger galvanized Melissa into rapidly scrabbling higher. She had gone only a few feet when she dropped one of her shoes and had to bend to retrieve it.

"Four," Evelyn counted. "Five. Six. Seven."

Melissa flew, her small teeth bared like those of a wolf cub that was exerting itself to its limit.

"Eight," Evelyn said, and raised the rock. "Nine."

Over the rise slid Melissa, terribly winded, her hands and knees chafed, the poncho rumpled and streaked with grass stains. "I don't like how you've been treating me," she spat resentfully. "I used to like you a lot, but I don't anymore."

"This isn't any easier for me." Evelyn tossed the rock to one side, moved to a log, and sat. "You can put your shoes on now."

"I thought you didn't want to leave any tracks?"

Evelyn was miffed and didn't answer. Here she was, doing her best to keep the two of them alive and out of the clutches of their abductors, and Melissa persisted in giving her a hard time every step of the way.

"I have blisters on my soles," Melissa said while tugging her first shoe on. "It'll hurt like the dickens when I walk."

"Do you ever do anything except gripe?" Evelyn asked. She finished and stood and stepped over the log. She had blisters, too, but Melissa didn't hear her complaining. The woods were a verdant labyrinth of predominantly pine buttressed by dense brush. How far the tableland ran, she couldn't say.

"I'm ready," Melissa announced, adjusting the poncho. Reaching underneath, she scratched furiously. "This thing is itching worse than ever. What if I have fleas?"

"Run," Evelyn said, and did so, jogging northwest. The important thing now was to cover as much ground as they could before the sun went down. Her leg muscles ached abominably for about fifty yards, but after that the pain faded.

Only a few minutes had gone by when Evelyn began to feel sickly. Nausea clawed at her innards, and she broke out in a cold sweat. The lack of food was to blame. She had to find something to eat by tomorrow morning or they would become too weak to go on.

Melissa had stopped complaining and was doggedly keeping up. "I'm sorry about back there," she said at one point. "It's just that I've never done anything like this before."

"Do you think I have?" Evelyn rejoined. She wasn't being entirely fair, though. She hadn't been born and bred back east, hadn't led the soft life Melissa had. She was older, stronger, tougher. She also had to be kinder. "I'm sorry, too. I really wouldn't have beaned you with that rock."

"They're real close, aren't they?" Melissa asked.

"Real close."

It was a race now, a race to keep ahead of Haro and Bittner until dark. The sun wouldn't set for several hours yet, and Evelyn knew that once the pair reached the top of the bluff they would come on swiftly. The only other thing she could think of to do was hide, but there wasn't anywhere they could hide that Haro wouldn't find them. So it was run or be taken captive again.

Evelyn's queasiness worsened. She had been pushing herself so hard for so long, her body was rebelling. A glance at Melissa showed she was feeling the same, if not worse. They'd wear themselves to a frazzle before too long—and be helpless to resist when Haro and Bittner overtook them.

"There has to be a way," Evelyn said grimly.

"How do you mean?" Melissa panted. She was starting to flag and had acquired a slight limp in her left leg.

Desperate, Evelyn scoured the woodland. Trees, trees, and more trees greeted her scrutiny. She raced on, but as the minutes passed she ran more and more slowly, a pain in her ribs compounding her worn condition. Just when she was ready to stop to catch her breath, they jogged into the open and before them broadened a wide basin heaped with deadfall. A cataclysm of nature, a severe storm or a chinook of cyclonic proportions, had flattened scores of trees, strewing them one on top of the other. In some places they were stacked five and six high, no two lying in the same position.

Evelyn smiled. "This is just what we needed." Deadfalls were the bane of mountain travel. Impassable to riders and a formidable obstacle to anyone on foot, they were invariably given a wide berth. No one in their right mind ever tried to go through one.

"How do you figure? It'll take us a month of Sundays to get through that tangle."

"Trust me," Evelyn said. Moving to the edge of the fall, she was afflicted by momentary doubt. The jumbled trees were heaped higher than a cabin and choked with broken limbs and new growth.

"Why are we doing this, exactly?" Melissa timorously inquired.

"Haro can't track us if there aren't any tracks," Evelyn said. Grasping a limb at chest height, she pulled herself up and climbed atop the first pile. Melissa had to give a little hop to reach the same limb, but once she had a handhold she scampered upward with the agility of a squirrel.

So far, so good, Evelyn thought. But as she soon discovered, penetrating deeper into the deadfall was a life-threatening proposition. More times than she cared to count they had to balance precariously on slender logs, or work their way hand over hand along branches that dangled over drops of twenty or thirty feet. Five minutes in, they came to a gap between a pair of pines lying at right angles on top of an even larger tree. Cracked and splintered limbs formed a partial roof that screened the opening from prying eyes.

"This will do us right fine." Gripping one of the limbs, Evelyn carefully lowered herself into the hole. There was ample room for her to sit with her back to one of the pines, and for Melissa to sit with her back to the other.

"How long are we staying here?" the smaller girl wanted to know.

"All night if need be." Evelyn's stomach growled in protest at the thought. A second later Melissa's stomach answered, and the two of them laughed merrily.

"I've always wondered what it would be like to starve to death," Melissa joked. "Now I reckon I'll get to find out."

Evelyn broke a small shoot off one of the branches overhead and held it out. "Gnaw on this awhile."

"You want me to eat a tree?" Melissa's mirth was contagious. "I'm a person, not a beaver."

"It won't kill you," Evelyn said. "Chew on the bark until it's pulp, then swallow." She selected a shoot for herself and stripped off the needles. The pine had a not-unpleasant minty taste.

Melissa nibbled at hers as if nibbling at an ear of corn. Scrunching her mouth, she remarked, "I don't see how you do it. I want to gag."

"I've eaten a lot worse."

Once, on a trek to the Pacific Ocean, Evelyn had been forced to eat grubs her mother found under a log. Another time, on the family's journey to Santa Fe, she had been treated to lizard, roasted rare.

"How you can live in these mountains is beyond me," Melissa said. "You're a lot braver than I am."

"Not necessarily."

"Oh, please. That bear. Killibrew's bunch. You've handled them all without batting an eye. You're at home here. I'm not, and never will be. Once I reach my uncle's plantation, I'm never leaving it."

"I'm just as at home in St. Louis," Evelyn said.

"Maybe so. But my father used to say everything has its natural element. Fish live in water. Bears live in the woods. Eagles have the sky." Melissa gnawed at the bark. "Your natural element are these mountains."

104

Evelyn scoffed at the notion. She had never felt at home in the wilds, and she couldn't see that she ever would. What did the wilderness have to offer besides a life of unending toil and a violent death? Few whites and Indians died in their sleep. Among the Shoshones, a nation more than five thousand strong, comparatively few lived to what whites would call a ripe old age. Being eaten by a bear or riddled by Blackfoot arrows wasn't how she wanted to end her days.

Melissa had more to say. "You know the animals, you know the land. You can do things other people can't. In St. Louis you'd be just another little girl. Nothing special about that."

"I don't want to be special. I want to be safe."

Stifling a yawn, Melissa said, "Safe how? From dying? Heck, in the States you can die as easily as out here. People get sick and keel over all the time. Accidents claim a lot, too. My grandfather fell from a moving wagon and had his neck broke."

"There aren't any grizzlies in North Carolina," Evelyn noted.

"So? We have rattlers and copperheads and cotton-mouths and coral snakes. We have footpads who will steal the clothes off your back, and brigands who will stab you for the coins in your purse. And others who will do a lot worse." Melissa yawned again. Their exertions were telling on her. "If you ask me, I don't think it's all that different from out here."

Evelyn was inclined to disagree, but a faint sound intruded, a gruff voice she pegged as Bittner's. Placing a finger to her lips, she rose high enough to peer out the opening. The 'breed and the bear were clambering across the deadfall in their general direction. She immediately ducked back down. "It's them!" she whispered. "Don't let out a peep."

The voices became louder. More sounds filtered down; the scrape of moccasins and boots, the creaking of limbs under great weight, the *crack* of a branch being broken.

"—sick and tired of this! Killibrew ain't going to like it. He ain't going to like it one bit."

"I have brought us this far," Haro said in his clipped, precise English. "We will catch them soon."

"You've been saying that since yesterday. Killibrew expected us to meet him at Buzzard Creek by noon. We're already five hours late." Bittner swore, and a fist smacked a palm. "You know how he gets when things don't work out how he wants. He'll take it out on me."

"It is the King girl," Haro said. "She is clever, that one. A worthy enemy."

Judging by their voices, they were twenty feet away and slightly to the left. Evelyn saw that Melissa had jammed a hand into her mouth and was hunched over in mortal terror.

"Enemy, my ass," Bittner declared. "She's a damned kid, for crying out loud. What is she? Eleven? And she's running us ragged. Try explaining that to Killibrew. He'll laugh in your face."

"This girl is not like others. She is part Shoshone, and her parents have taught her well. She thinks and acts as a warrior would. Or as a hunter, like her father."

"She's still just a *kid*," Bittner said in exasperation. "You have some nerve calling yourself a tracker when she's outwitted you every step of the way."

Haro's tone implied that he disliked the veiled insult. "If Killibrew or you can do better, then you do the tracking."

"Don't get touchy on me," Bittner said. "I'm just telling you how things are." He indulged in a flurry of cusswords. Nearby branches rustled, followed by a thump. "Ahhh. This is more like it. Make yourself comfortable while I light my pipe."

"We waste daylight," Haro said.

"Taken a gander at the sun lately? There ain't much left. We've lost the scent and might as well call it a day."

"They are here somewhere. I can feel them. If we keep searching—"

Bittner snorted in derision. "Oh, sure. How many acres are we talking about? Fifteen? Twenty? It shouldn't take us more than a year or two to poke around in every nook and cranny." He patted a log. "Take a load off. We'll make camp in the woods yonder and start looking again at first light."

A shadow flicked across the opening. Evelyn recoiled, fearing the half-breed had found them. Instead, the log above Melissa sagged to the weight of someone sitting down.

"You've got to learn to relax," Bittner chided. "In the whole time I've known you, I haven't seen you laugh once."

"What is there to laugh about?" Haro said. "That we are born, we live, and we die? That maggots will feast on our bodies and our bones will rot away?"

"God Almighty," Bittner said. "No wonder you have such a sour disposition. Didn't your ma or pa ever tell you life is meant for living?"

"My father was mutilated and scalped by Sioux when I had seen but four winters. My mother was out gathering firewood a winter later and was caught in a blizzard. They did not find her frozen body until the next spring."

"Tarnation. You're depressing as hell, you know that?" A match rasped, and the aroma of tobacco drifted down through the latticed limbs. "We all have sob stories to tell. The trick is not to dwell on them."

"Life is life," Haro said.

"And piss stinks. So what? Me, I don't fret myself over things I can't change. I make the best of what is thrown my way. It's all any of us can do."

Evelyn heard Bittner puff on his pipe. Smoky tendrils seeped into their hiding place and her nose began to tingle.

"I just hope this King fella delivers the gold like we want." Bittner waxed talkative. "I'm taking my share and heading for parts unknown. I'll shave and get me a fancy set of clothes so no one can recognize me and live in luxury for as long as the gold lasts." More puffing ensued, then: "What do you aim to do with your share?"

"I want to buy a hat."

"A hat? Killibrew says we'll end up with five to ten thousand dollars apiece, and all you want is a stupid hat?"

"I saw it at Bent's Fort. It is red with black ribbons, and has spiderwebs in front."

"Spiderwebs? Are you talking about that one on the shelf behind the cracker barrel? The one with the feather?"

"That is the one," Haro confirmed.

Bittner roared with laughter. "That's a woman's hat! Those spiderwebs, as you call 'em, is what we call lace."

"No one in my tribe has a hat like that. When I go back, my people will look on me with respect."

"They'll look on you as a mule's butt," Bittner said. "If you really want to impress them, buy a new horse and saddle. And a bunch of trinkets for the ladies."

"I have no interest in finding a wife."

"Who said anything about getting hitched? You can milk a cow without buying it. With all the gold you're going to have, the females won't care what color your skin is."

More acrid smoke drifted into the cavity. Evelyn pinched her nose to suppress a cough and saw Melissa imitate her.

"Yes, sir," Bittner crowed. "We'll be rolling in nuggets. That is, if we can count on Killibrew to divide it up as he promised."

"Why wouldn't he?"

"With that much gold at stake, you have to ask? He never has been much on sharing. I wouldn't put it past him to double-cross us and keep it all for himself."

"He could only do that if he killed us."

"You catch on quick," Bittner said.

Haro shifted, his right foot sliding along a branch only a couple of feet above Melissa. "Of all of us, you know him best. You have ridden with him for five winters. Yet you do not trust him?"

"No further than I can fling Long's Peak, no," Bittner said. "We're pards, true, but that wouldn't stop him from putting a slug in my back when I wasn't looking if it got him my share of the nuggets."

"I will not turn my back on him, then."

Melissa had both hands over her beet-red face and was rocking up and down in distress. Evelyn slid toward her but stopped when another shadow rippled across the gap. Afraid one of the men had spotted the opening, she glanced up.

"You'll have to do more than that," Bittner confided. "Don't drink or eat anything he gives you."

"Why not?"

The log above Melissa bent lower still.

"I shouldn't be telling you this, but Killibrew got his hands on some poison when we were in New Orleans last year. The kind they use to kill those big rats down on the docks." Bittner lowered his voice confidentially. "He might try to do us in by mixing some in with our food or water."

"Why do you tell me this?" Haro asked suspiciously. "You hardly know me."

"I need someone to watch my back, and I can't trust the kid to do it. He's too green, too wet behind the ears. You, though, hardly ever sleep, and you're cautious as can be. So how about if you watch my back and I watch yours? We might get through this alive."

For some reason the smoke was growing worse by the second. Evelyn's eyes were stinging, and she couldn't take a breath, even a shallow one, without inhaling the stuff and wanting to cough. Squinting to keep it out of her eyes, she spied a small black object jutting between the limbs above Melissa. It was the bowl of Bittner's pipe. He had lowered it when he bent toward Haro.

Melissa doubled over, tears streaming down her chipmunk cheeks, her thumbs pinching her nose. Her chest was

David Thompson

heaving, but she courageously held herself perfectly still and didn't make a sound.

Evelyn crept toward her, wrapped an arm around Melissa's shoulders, and began to slide her toward the other side where the smoke wasn't quite as heavy. They had to pass under the pipe, and as they did a tiny burning ember slid over the lip and fell onto her neck.

Automatically, Evelyn threw back her head to cry out. By sheer force of will she smothered the pain and the yelp died in her throat. They slid a few more inches, their feet noiseless on the smooth bole. A puff of fresh air through the opening dispelled some of the smoke, and Evelyn breathed a little easier. She smiled at Melissa, who had straightened.

"How do I know this is not a trick?" Haro asked.

"What would be the purpose?" Bittner rejoined. "If you tell Killibrew what I've told you, he'll blow my brains out. I'm taking a chance confiding in you, and I hope to hell you take me serious."

"I will think on your words."

"Don't think too long. I have a feeling we'll catch these brats sooner than we expect."

Evelyn felt a convulsive ripple flow through Melissa. Too late, she saw that Melissa's mouth was wide open. The next instant the younger girl let out with a horrendous sneeze.

Chapter Nine

Ezriah Hampton wasn't the world's best tracker. He couldn't tell individual tracks, one from the other, unless it was glaringly obvious. He couldn't tell how old tracks were except as a general guess. He couldn't tell the speed at which the maker of the tracks was going, or determine the weight or sex. So it was fortunate for him that the four horses he was tracking left enough sign even he could shadow them for miles on end without losing the trail.

For most of the day that trail led due north. Only once did Ezriah stop, at a stream at midday. The kidnappers had done likewise, and Ezriah scoured the soft earth for footprints. He located the tracks of two men, but none made by the girls. It puzzled him. Surely Killibrew had let them climb down to drink? He spent more time than he should going over the area a second and even a third time, but the result was always the same.

Confused, Ezriah climbed onto the sorrel and rode on. He wondered if Killibrew had already disposed of Evelyn and Melissa and buried them along the way. Yet if that were the case, he'd have spotted the graves. Mounds of upturned earth would stick out like proverbial sore thumbs. Or could it be that Killibrew had rolled the bodies down the mountain and left them for scavengers to dispose of?

The thought filled Ezriah with apprehension.

After leaving the stream, Killibrew had traveled in a northwesterly direction and availed himself of heavy cover where it was available, a precaution against being spotted by hostiles, Ezriah figured.

Ezriah assumed the cutthroats would continue on until sunset, so he was quite surprised when, along about four in the afternoon, he crossed a rise and saw smoke from a campfire rising ahead. Sliding from the saddle, he looped the chestnut's reins around a sapling and glided forward through heavy timber until he heard voices.

In a clearing beside a narrow creek Killibrew had called a halt. The four horses were tethered in a string, and the youngest kidnapper, Kyle, was gathering more wood for the fire Killibrew was tending. Ezriah didn't see Bittner or the 'breed. Nor, to his chagrin, did he see the girls.

"God, no," Ezriah breathed, fearing the worst had come to pass. He started to lift his rifle, then decided to listen to what the two men were saying before he did anything. Easing onto his belly, he snaked from bush to bush until he was near enough to eavesdrop.

Killibrew was squatting and gazing westward, tapping a hand on the rifle across his thighs as if he were mad. When Kyle deposited another armload of firewood, Killibrew brusquely snapped, "Damn them all to hell! They should have been here by now."

"Maybe it's taking longer than you reckoned," the younger man said.

"To catch a couple of brats?" Killibrew snorted. "They're grown men. Haro is one of the best trackers alive. How damn long could it take?"

"Maybe they're having trouble finding Buzzard Creek, then," Kyle suggested.

Killibrew jerked a thumb at the gently gurgling waterway, half the width of the previous stream and only six inches deep at most. "We found it, didn't we? And Haro knows this country a hell of a lot better than we do." He shifted, facing west. "No, something must be wrong. It could be they ran into hostiles. At Bent's Fort we were told a war party attacked a wagon train bound for the Oregon country about a month ago, not all that far north of here."

Kyle nervously fingered one of the flintlocks at his waist. "So the war party could still be in the area?"

"Relax, boy. No use in givin' yourself an ulcer. When a man's time comes, it comes, and there ain't a damn thing he can do to change it."

Ezriah digested the information. Amazingly, it sounded to him as if Evelyn and Melissa had escaped, and the 'breed and Bittner had been sent to bring them back. *Good for you, girls!* he thought with a grin. They had sand to spare.

"What if they never show up?" Kyle asked.

"Then you and me will go on to the Missouri and wait for Nate King to show," Killibrew answered. "There will be that much more gold for us to split."

"But we don't have his daughters."

"He won't know that, will he? We'll tell him they're off somewhere safe, and he can't see them until we're sure he's brought the gold. We'll offer him some coffee, and that will be that. He'll be dead and we'll be rich."

"One of us is going to shoot him in the back when his back is turned?" Kyle said, his tone implying that he didn't approve.

"It's a hell of a lot safer to shoot someone in the back than in the front," Killibrew responded. "Leave the killin' to me. I'm not as squeamish as you. King will be dead before he knows it, and we won't need to lift a finger."

David Thompson

Ezriah debated what his next step should be. He had a powerful hankering to core Killibrew's noggin with a slug. The boy's, too, if it came to that. But if Bittner and the 'breed showed up with the girls and hailed the camp, as was customary, and didn't receive an answer, they might skedaddle and take Evelyn and Melissa with them. Or shoot the girls, then light a shuck.

Ezriah decided not to kill the pair just yet. He had time to spare. He hadn't seen any sign of the Kings on his back trail all day, so he must be a couple of hours ahead of them. They wouldn't arrive until after dark. Folding his arms, he rested his chin on a wrist and settled down to wait.

Nate King and Winona reached the shelf on the far side of the pass shortly after sunrise, and Nate climbed down to read sign. The tracks of the chestnut Hampton had appropriated, imposed over those of the kidnappers, showed where the old-timer had gone off after Killibrew and Kyle.

Of much more interest to Nate were Evelyn's and Melissa's prints. He tracked them into the trees below, Winona following and leading the bay and the mare. "They got away!" he announced, his fatherly pride at his daughter's bold audacity tempered by his woodsman's knowledge of the potential perils they faced.

"That is my daughter," Winona said with a smile.

Another set of footprints paralleled those of the girls. "The half-breed and the big one went after them on foot," Nate informed her.

"Haro and Bittner, Ezriah called them." Winona hunkered to examine the prints herself. "We have a good chance of catching up to them before sunset, husband."

That they did. As Nate accepted the bay's reins and turned to the saddle, a thought struck him. "Ezriah doesn't realize the girls escaped. That's why he went on after Killibrew and the other one."

114

"He can use the exercise," Winona said, uncurling. "He's the laziest man I have ever met. All he does is lounge around our cabin, eating our pantry bare."

"He's putting himself in danger for no reason."

"That is not our concern." Winona climbed onto her mare. "We did not ask him to go after them. He did it on his own."

"To help us out," Nate said. "To make up for letting them be taken in the first place." He respected Ezriah for that, and felt a sense of obligation to keep the old man from getting himself killed.

"You are only guessing at his motive," Winona said curtly. She hiked her reins. "Why are you standing there? Our daughter needs us."

Nate forked leather but didn't ride off. "One of us should go after Ezriah."

Winona's astonishment, under different circumstances, would have been comical. "Our daughter is in danger and you worry about *him*?" she bristled. "Go help him if you want, but I am not resting until Blue Flower is safe in my arms."

"I'm the one who should go after the girls," Nate said. "I'm a better tracker." It was the sensible thing to do.

"You want *me* to follow Ezriah?" Winona looked at him, and looked at him, and finally said, "Do you listen when I speak? Or are you one of those husbands who shuts his ears whenever his wife opens her mouth? I do not like Hampton. He is arrogant and obnoxious. He looks down his nose at me because I am a woman, and in his eyes women are lesser than men. He mocks and teases me without cease. To be honest, husband, I do not care whether he lives or dies."

"You'll do it, then?" Nate said.

Winona was a full minute answering. "When this is over, you and I will sit down and have a long talk."

Kneeing the bay alongside the mare, Nate leaned over and kissed her on the cheek. "It's the right thing to do."

"In your eyes. In mine, I hate you at this moment, and I have never hated you before, no matter how mad you made me." Winona transferred her Hawken to her left hand and reined the mare northward. "When you find my bleached bones a moon from now, remember whose idea this was."

"I'll rejoin you as soon as I can," Nate promised, and without glancing back he trotted down the next slope and on into a belt of spruce. In order to locate Evelyn as quickly as possible, he had to take shortcuts where possible. The footprints were bearing to the northwest, which told him his daughter was making for his son's cabin. Rather than parallel them all the way down, as Haro and Bittner had done, he rode as fast as the terrain allowed until he came to the bottom near where he believed Evelyn and Melissa had come out and scoured the ground for more sign. Within minutes he found their tracks and soon reached a stream.

The huge prints of a grizzly gave Nate pause. Hopping down, he made sure that neither of the girls had been harmed. When he saw where Evelyn had stared the bear down, just as he had taught her, her courage brought a tightness to his chest and moisture to his eyes.

Fording the stream, Nate took up the chase anew. On horseback he could travel three times as fast as a man on foot, and he had high hopes of being reunited with Evelyn long before sundown. Then he reached the spot where the girls had removed their shoes.

Drawing rein, Nate mulled his options. From horseback their prints were now impossible to read. Those of Bittner and Haro, however, were still as plain as ever. He could follow theirs instead, but if they lost the trail, he'd need to backtrack, delaying him who knew how long. His best bet was to continue to the northwest at a gallop and look for sign only when he had to.

A flick of the reins and Nate was off. Time slipped by. The vegetation thinned. On his right a bluff appeared. He was about to ride past when he played a hunch. Long ago

116

he had taught Evelyn to use the terrain to her advantage, and instructed her that when it came to evading an enemy, whether human or otherwise, gaining high ground was the smart thing to do.

From the top of that bluff Evelyn could see for miles. So, on the assumption she had found a way up, Nate conducted a brief search. In bare earth near a game trail he found what he was looking for: the faint impressions of small stockinged feet. Superimposed over them were the tracks of the half-breed's moccasins and the thick-soled boots worn by Bittner.

The trail posed a problem for the bay. In places it was hazardously steep, and for most of its length it was barely wide enough for an animal the bay's size. Two-thirds of the way up, Nate swung off and walked. Several times the bay slipped, but it never fell, and presently Nate attained the summit.

Large outlines revealed where Evelyn and Melissa had slept. On awakening, they had gone up another steep slope to a wooded tableland. Nate estimated that he was only two hours behind, if that, and once he established that they were still heading northwest, he galloped headlong on their heels.

Periodically, images of Winona filled Nate's head and pangs of guilt assailed him. He had done what was best, of that he was certain, and although he had no regrets, he couldn't blame his wife for being peeved. He would have been were the situation reversed.

"It won't be long," Nate said to the bay.

They came to a broad basin carved from the tableland millennia ago. Deadfall covered it now, a twisted maze of downed trees of all types and sizes, impenetrable on horseback and nearly so on foot. A brief examination established that Evelyn and Melissa had braved the jumbled mass, and that Haro and Bittner had gone in after them.

Nate had to hand it to his youngest. She was demonstrating remarkable wilderness savvy. Removing her shoes, going for the high ground, and now seeking cover in the deadfall were extremely clever tactics. He had to remember to compliment her when they were reunited.

Rising in the stirrups, Nate scanned the basin for sign of the 'breed and the other cutthroat. Either they had heard the bay and hidden—or they were gone. He moved along the edge of the deadfall, hoping he wouldn't find what he soon did: footprints leading from the basin into the woods to the northeast. Four sets of footprints—those of the men *and* those of Evelyn and Melissa.

The girls had been recaptured. Nate was now only fifteen or twenty minutes behind, though, and on horseback he could overhaul them in no time. Smiling in keen anticipation, he goaded the bay to a gallop and plunged into the leafy timberland.

Bittner hadn't stopped chuckling since he reached into the cavity in the deadfall and yanked Melissa out of the hole by her hair. "Sitting there right under our noses the whole damn time!" he declared, and slapped his thigh in merriment. "If it wasn't for that sneeze, we'd never have suspected."

Melissa flushed at the mention, looked at Evelyn, and said softly, "I'm sorry. It's all my fault."

"Blame his pipe," Evelyn said.

At this Bittner cackled anew. He was in extraordinarily fine spirits and was treating them in a much more friendly fashion than he had before they escaped.

Evelyn attributed it to relief. Bittner had been afraid of Killibrew's wrath if Haro and he returned empty-handed. Although the bearded giant was twice Killibrew's size, Evelyn suspected that Bittner was scared to death of him. And after overhearing that business about the poison, she knew why.

Haro was in the lead, moving as silently as a specter, never talking unless spoken to. Every so often he looked behind them. The next time he did, his dark eyes narrowed and he slowed. He stared a bit, then hiked on.

"Anything wrong?" Bittner asked.

"I thought I saw something."

Evelyn twisted her head. Other than a vagrant butterfly in search of a mountain meadow and a flock of sparrows gamboling in a thicket, nothing was back there. "Where are you taking us?" she demanded.

"You'll find out soon enough, girly," Bittner replied. To the Pawnee he said, "Let's hope to hell Killibrew is where he's supposed to be. He's not the most patient cuss on the planet. When we didn't show on time, he might have gone on alone with Kyle." He paused. "More gold for them that way."

Haro didn't reply, so Evelyn did instead. "That's some friend you have. Why did you hook up with a man who would stab you in the back as soon as look at you? Or poison you, if it suits him?"

Bittner's craggy features clouded. "You heard me back yonder, did you?" A long stride brought him abreast of her, and he gripped her roughly by the throat. "Listen, girl, and listen good. If you say one word of what you heard to Killibrew, I'll deny it. And when you least expect, I'll snap your scrawny neck like a twig."

Evelyn wasn't the least bit afraid. "You won't lay a finger on me until after you have the gold."

"Think so, do you?" Bittner's thumb and forefinger closed like a vise on her neck and he lifted her bodily off the ground.

Evelyn's breath was choked off before she could fill her lungs, and pain spiked her chest. Flailing her legs, she beat at his muscular arms with her small fists, but they were ineffectual.

"Accidents happen, girl," Bittner said. "So long as we have one of you brats, your pa ain't likely to buck us. And we'll still have your sister."

Melissa leaped at him and beat at his stout legs, but her blows had no more effect than Evelyn's. "Put her down, you brute! Harm her and you'll never get the gold! She's Nate King's daughter, not me!"

Bittner's hairy eyebrows met over his brutish eyes. "What's that?"

"I'm Melissa Braddock, not Melissa King. Evelyn and her folks saved me from a war party, and I've been living with them until my uncle gets here from North Carolina." Melissa said it in a rush.

"The hell you say." Bittner had forgotten about Evelyn. His thick fingers wedged in her flesh, he bent over Melissa. "We've been hauling you all over creation and you're not even a King?"

Melissa shook her head.

"How do I know you're telling the truth?"

"Ask Evelyn," Melissa said.

Bittner glanced at Evelyn's red face, blinked as if surprised he was still choking her, and let go.

Gasping for air, Evelyn tumbled onto a shoulder. Her throat was throbbing, her lungs fit to burst. She rocked back and forth in agony. Gradually, it subsided, and as it did she heard raucous laughter.

Bittner was doubled over, his ham-sized hands on his knees. "Don't this beat all, Haro? All this time we thought they were sisters! Killibrew will be fit to be tied."

Rolling onto her knees, Evelyn croaked, "You're not going to tell him." Given Killibrew's violent nature, she suspected he might abandon Melissa in the wilderness—or worse.

"Oh?" Bittner said, and laughed some more. "Why would that be?"

"Because if you tell him about her, I'll tell him what you told Haro."

The bearded outlaw straightened, his dander up. "Who the hell do you think you are to be threatening me? You're

120

a snot-nosed kid, is what. I'll do as I damn well please. And you'll do as I damn well want you to."

"Do we have a deal?" Evelyn asked.

Bittner's response was to level his rifle so the muzzle touched Melissa's temple. "I can blow out her wick right here and Killibrew wouldn't hold it against me. And I can cut your tongue out so you can't blab. How would that be?" he taunted.

Evelyn remembered a trip back east to visit friends. A girl slightly older than she had delighted in pushing her around every chance she got, and Evelyn had gone to her father and asked for advice. She didn't want to hurt the girl, but she couldn't stand being bullied. "People like her only understand one thing," her father said. "You can talk to her until you're blue in the face and she won't change. You have to stand up to her, show her she can't buffalo you." He had tenderly ruffled her hair. "Sad to say, but those who like to hurt people only back down when they think you'll hurt them."

Evelyn met Bittner's glare with one of her own. "Cut out my tongue and my pa will cut out yours. Harm Melissa and you'll be a long time dying." She smiled knowingly. "Ever seen what Indians do to their enemies? Ever seen a white man staked out to die? They gouge out the eyes and cut off the fingers, nose, and ears. Then they wait for the ants to come. Or maybe coyotes."

Bittner's belligerence withered like a plant under a scorching sun. "You don't scare me none," he said, his expression belying his statement. Lowering the rifle, he pushed Melissa at Evelyn. "So she's not your sister. What do I care? So long as she doesn't cause me grief, I won't say a thing."

Evelyn hugged Melissa, then noticed Haro giving her the most peculiar look. Not a friendly look, but not unfriendly, either. More as if he were impressed by something, although she was at a loss as to how she could have impressed a man like him.

"Head out," Bittner barked.

Melissa clasped Evelyn's hand as they walked. "Thank you. You're the bravest girl I've ever met."

"No braver than you. You stood up to him when he was strangling me." Evelyn rubbed her sore throat.

"I wish we'd met some other place, some other time," Melissa said. "I bet we'd be wonderful friends."

"I thought we already were."

Melissa's eyes teared over, and she dabbed at them with the blanket. "My pa was right, as always."

"About what?"

"That you and your family are as nice as can be. It was that day the Indians attacked. He took me aside and told me he wanted me to go with your father so I'd be safe. I didn't want to. I cried. I begged him. But Pa wouldn't listen. He said that one of us had to get out alive, and that he'd rather it was me as I was the youngest."

Evelyn gave her a reassuring squeeze. "Your father was a brave man."

"He said I had the most to live for. That I should do him proud and have a family of my own one day. I told him I thought boys are pigs and I'd never marry, and he just laughed."

"I used to think that when I was your age," Evelyn said. Before her brother married and the miracle occurred.

Melissa gazed skyward. "If my pa is looking down from heaven, I hope he knows I'll do my best to make him proud. I do have an awful lot to live for."

"We all do."

Haro glanced back again, but not at them. He gazed intently westward, and tensed. Halting, he turned completely around, his posture like that of a wolf that has caught the scent of deer.

"What the devil has gotten into you?" Bittner demanded.

"Someone is on our trail."

"Where?" Bittner spun and raised his rifle. He stared a minute, then grated, "You're seeing things. I don't see anyone."

"Keep watching. He is far back yet."

Could it be? Evelyn's pulse jumped. She pivoted and probed the woods, but to her immense disappointment she saw no one.

"It's just one man?" Bittner was swinging his rifle from side to side, seeking a target to shoot.

"Just one. A white man on a black horse."

Evelyn's father rode a black horse, a bay he'd owned for years. She looked again, with the same result.

"You're crazy," Bittner grumbled. "Your eyes must be playing tricks on you. I still don't see him."

"My full Pawnee name means 'He Who Has Eyes of Hawk,' " Haro said a trifle indignantly. He took a step, and suddenly pointed. "There! Do your weak eyes see him now? Crossing that clearing?"

At the limit of Evelyn's vision a stick figure materialized— a rider, sure enough—and while he was too far off to say who he was with any certainty, his horse was indeed black. He hadn't spotted them yet, and wouldn't until he was a lot closer.

Bittner's mouth creased in a vicious smirk. "I'll be damned. It must be Nate King, come to rescue the blood of his blood." Winking at Evelyn, he cocked his rifle. "I reckon he didn't take our hemp lesson to heart, girl. Now we'll have to teach him the error of his ways." Bittner grabbed her by the arm. "And you're the perfect bait to bring him right into our sights."

Chapter Ten

Serpentine tendrils of smoke curled skyward over the next rise. Winona King drew rein, licked a finger, and held it aloft. The wind was blowing from the northwest to the southeast. Accordingly, she reined to the right and rode along the rise until she was downwind of whoever was responsible for the campfire.

Three possibilities sprang to Winona's mind: It was the old trapper, the kidnappers, or a band of Indians. The last she tended to discount; Indians had too much sense to build a fire that large. There was a saying among the Shoshones and other tribes to the effect that Indians made small fires and ended their journeys in their own lodges, while white men made big fires and ended their journeys with their scalps decorating the walls of Blackfoot lodges.

Her Hawken across her legs, Winona cautiously guided the mare through thick pines until she spied two figures seated beside a fire near Buzzard Creek, as the whites called it. Based on the descriptions Hampton had provided, she identified the pair as Killibrew and Kyle. A cold fury seized her. Killibrew was the leader of the men who had abducted her daughter. Of all of them, he was the most to blame. Of all of them, he was the one she most wanted to slay.

Halting behind a spruce, Winona slid off and looped the reins around a limb. She doubled over and slunk forward until she was on her stomach behind a cottonwood thirty feet from the unsuspecting kidnappers. A fragrant aroma reached her. They were drinking hot chocolate, of all things.

". . . better have a damn good reason for being so late," Killibrew was saying. "We'll give them until morning. If they haven't shown by then, we'll head for the rendezvous site."

"Wouldn't it be better to go look for them?" Kyle said between sips. "I still say they ran into hostiles. Or maybe a griz." He surveyed the primeval landscape to the west. "Out here anything can happen."

"Don't lecture me on life in the wilderness, pup," Killibrew said sourly. "I was huntin' coons and such before you were wearin' diapers."

"I didn't mean any insult."

"If I thought you had, I'd have slit you like a fish." Killibrew grinned wickedly. "There's something you'd better learn, boy, and learn it right now. Out here it's every coyote for himself. Sure, we're workin' together, but that doesn't make us friends. Once we have the gold, we'll go our separate ways and likely never set eyes on one another again."

Kyle lowered his tin cup to his lap. "I'd rather you didn't call me 'boy.' And even if what you say is true, there's no reason we can't be civil as long as we're together."

"Civil?" Killibrew tittered. "Where the hell do you reckon you are? Among polite society?" He gestured in contempt. "In the wilds it's kill or be killed. A fella has to be hard as an anvil to survive. If you're not, others take that as weakness, and they'll prey on you like a pack of wolves on sheep."

David Thompson

"That old-timer and those girls were nice enough until they found out what we were up to," Kyle said.

"Are you addlepated? That old geezer tumbled to us the moment he laid eyes on us. He wanted to whisk the brats to their parents, but we outfoxed him." Killibrew fed a small limb to the fire. "I was watchin' his eyes. He almost went for his guns. If we hadn't outnumbered him, if he'd thought those girls had any hope at all of getting away, he'd gladly have gone down shootin' if it bought them time to make it home."

Winona glanced to her left. Ezriah Hampton had to be close by, spying on the two men as she was doing. She still couldn't forgive him for letting the girls be taken, but her resentment dropped several notches.

"He sure was a spooky cuss," Kyle commented. "With that eye of his, and all those wrinkles, he looked as if he'd just popped out of a grave."

"If we ever see that old bastard again, it'll be the other way around," Killibrew declared. "I'll blow out his wick, permanent-like."

"You like to kill, don't you?" the younger man observed.

"I don't mind it none," Killibrew replied. "I was twelve when I shot my first man, a darkie who had the gall to mouth off to me when I pushed him. After that it was a Delaware who had a rifle I took a hankerin' to."

"How many have you rubbed out, altogether?"

"I don't keep count, boy. It would be like counting how many flies you've swatted." Killibrew tilted his head back and drained the last of his hot chocolate. For a few moments he stared at the cottonwoods concealing Winona, but she was confident he couldn't see her. Then he set the cup down on a flat rock, stiffly rose, and stretched. "We need to refill the coffeepot. I'll be right back." Pot in hand, he ambled toward the creek.

Kyle appeared surprised by something but didn't say anything. He stared after the moonfaced killer, then gazed

126

rather wistfully eastward. Perhaps he missed the life he had forsaken. Or perhaps he was reflecting on loved ones he had left behind.

Winona watched Killibrew until he came to a high bank and jumped down the other side. She lost sight of him and turned her attention to the surrounding woodland. *Where is Hampton?* In that outlandish outfit of his he should be easy to spot, but although she probed every clump of brush and every shadow, she couldn't locate him.

Kyle opened a pair of saddlebags and sorted through the contents.

Aligning the Hawken's sights on the young man's chest, Winona touched her finger to the trigger. But she didn't fire. She couldn't make up her mind whether to shoot them where they sat or wait until dark, take them alive, and kill them at her leisure. They deserved to die. No question of that. She wanted to see Killibrew's face when she shot him. She wanted him to know it was coming.

Kyle had unwrapped a cloth and was holding a silver locket. Opening it, he grew sad, and touched a fingertip to whatever the locket contained. A miniature portrait, Winona guessed. She had seen other whites carry them.

Killibrew was taking his sweet time. Winona scanned the bank and wondered what was keeping him. He was in need of a bath, but she doubted bathing was high on the list of things he liked to do. She listened for splashing sounds, for the scrape of the coffeepot on a rock, but heard only muted gurgling.

A hoof stamped behind her.

Twisting, Winona discovered that the mare's reins had come undone, and the mare had followed her and was standing in the open where the kidnappers might see. One already had.

Killibrew's stroll to the creek had been a ruse. He was ten feet away, a cocked pistol pointed at her midsection.

"Well, what have we here?" he said, and grinned. "You'd be Nate King's squaw, I gather?"

Winona's rifle was pointed toward their camp. She couldn't possibly whirl and fire before he did, and at that close range he couldn't miss. She was mad at her lapse, mad she hadn't realized the mare was there sooner.

"Answer me, damn you," Killibrew said, taking a step. "If you think I won't shoot, you're mistaken."

Winona was under no such illusion. "Yes, your assumption is correct. I am Nate King's wife."

"My assumption?" Chortling, Killibrew came closer. "Hell, woman, you speak English better than me. And you're a looker, to boot. I never met your hubby, but he has fine taste in females."

"The day you do meet him will be your last," Winona pronounced.

"Is that so? Could be I'll have the last laugh, not him." Killibrew sidled to his left and warily relieved her of the Hawken. "Here's what I want you to do. Nice and slow, get on your knees and toss your belt hardware over by your critter. The same with that pigsticker. Then put your hands behind your head and keep them there."

Choking down her resentment, Winona reached for one of her pistols.

"Nice and slow!" Killibrew stressed. "I know how damned tricky you squaws can be. I lost a friend to a Cheyenne squaw once. We were diddlin' her, and she pulled a knife we never saw until it was stickin' between his ribs."

"It is unfortunate she didn't stick you, too," Winona commented, slowly wrapping her fingers around the flintlock. If only he would blink or glance away. But his gaze and his gun were rock-steady. She threw the flintlock into the grass and lowered her hand to the other one.

"Yes, sir," Killibrew said, ogling her, a gleam in his eyes that hadn't been there moments before. "The more I study on you, the more I admire. You're a fine filly. Got a body like a ripe plum."

"Lay a hand on me and I will scratch your eyes out."

"Funny. That Cheyenne gal said the same thing. And I left her breathing her own blood after I jiggered her silly."

Winona slowly eased the second pistol from under her belt. She sorely wanted to flip back the hammer and snap off a shot, but she tossed it after the first.

"Now the pigsticker, bitch," Killibrew directed, growing more smug with each weapon she discarded.

Her blood boiling, Winona complied. Placing her hands behind her head, she waited for him to come close enough for her to spring.

The short hardcase visibly relaxed. "That wasn't so hard, was it?" he bated her. "Stand up so I can get a better look at that body of yours." A low whistle fluttered from his lips. "My, oh my. You are enough to make a man's mouth water. Maybe I'll have to rethink my opinion of squaws."

"Go to hell."

Killibrew laughed, and his pistol dipped a whisker. "I like gals with fire. I bet you're a regular wildcat under the sheets. I bet you scratch and claw and caterwaul your lungs out, huh?"

Winona averted her face as if in shame, but under her hooded lids she watched his flintlock. Its muzzle dipped lower as he cackled on at her expense and took another step. Instantly she leaped, her hands formed into talons, but suddenly she was staring down the barrel of his weapon.

"That's far enough," Killibrew warned. "What do you take me for? A greenhorn?"

The undergrowth crackled, and through it plowed Kyle. "What on earth is going on? I heard a commotion and—" He saw Winona and drew up short. "Good Lord! Where did she come from?"

"Where do you think?" Killibrew rejoined. "Meet Mrs. Nate King, come to rescue her brood. Only, she wasn't as clever as she thought she was."

129

Kyle anxiously scoured the woods on both sides. "If she's here, her husband must be, too. What do we do?"

"We stay calm, for starters," Killibrew said. "If the squaw lover were here, he'd have shown himself by now. I have a hunch he went after Bittner and Haro and sent her to keep an eye on us. It's a mistake that'll cost him."

"What are you fixing to do?" Kyle asked.

"Make the lady comfortable. While I'm at it, fetch her horse and her weapons. Tie the nag with ours."

Kyle studied her, but with none of the lechery Killibrew exhibited. "She's awful pretty. I can see a lot of her in the oldest girl, Evelyn."

"Pick her flowers, why don't you?" Killibrew jested. To Winona he said in a gravelly growl, "Do exactly as I tell you, woman. Walk to the fire with your hands on your head and kneel in front of it. Don't stop. Don't turn. Or else."

The indignity of being caught was compounded by Winona's knowledge that the moment she stepped into the open, Ezriah Hampton would know she had fallen into their clutches. Holding her chin high, she marched from the trees.

"I like how your hips sway," Killibrew complimented her. "That dress of yours is too loose, though. You should tighten it some to show off those legs." He paused. "That is, if you were going to live that long."

Winona twisted her head and glared at him.

"I warned you," Killibrew said, and fired.

Ezriah Hampton had dozed off. His lack of sleep the night before and the arduous ride had conspired to lull him into laying his forehead on his arm. He only intended to rest his eyes a bit, but the next thing he knew, he heard voices and he looked up to behold Winona King being ushered toward the campfire at gunpoint by Killibrew. Dumbfounded, Ezriah thought he must be imagining it. But there was no denying the reality of the shot that boomed, nor Killibrew's sadistic glee.

For a heart-stopping moment Ezriah thought the bastard had shot Winona King dead. But no, Killibrew had fired past her head, then drawn his other pistol before she could capitalize.

Kyle came rushing from the pines. He was leading Winona's mare, his arms burdened by her hardware. "What was the shot for?"

"I was learnin' the squaw to heed her betters," Killibrew said. "Like her old man, she's got rocks between her ears."

Winona had recoiled at the blast and covered her left ear with her hand. The pistol had gone off practically in her face, and she had black smudges on her cheeks and forehead. "You might have ruptured my eardrum!" she snapped.

"Trust me. That's the least of your worries," Killibrew responded, and waved her on to the fire. As she folded onto her knees, he moved around until he was directly across from her and squatted. "Now, then. Suppose we have us a palaver before the fun begins. Was I right about your husband going after Bittner and the 'breed?"

Ezriah saw Winona smirk.

"Clammin' up on me, eh? I can loosen your tongue if I have to." To demonstrate, Killibrew trained his pistol on her leg. "Ever seen someone shot in the knee? I have. It hurts like hell. They scream and blubber and carry on something awful."

"I will not tell you a thing," Winona defied him.

Kyle deposited her firearms well out of her reach and moved toward the horse string with her mare. "She might be of use to us alive," he remarked. "To bargain with if her husband makes it this far."

Killibrew mulled the suggestion a few moments and slowly lowered his flintlock. "The boy has a point," he said, more to himself than to either of them. "There isn't a man

131

alive who can outfox the 'breed, but better safe than sorry."

Ezriah was mightily pleased that Winona had been spared, even if only temporarily. Now he had to get her out of there before her independent streak reaped a lead ball between the eyes. To his right the ground was more open than he liked; to his left was ample cover that passed within spitting distance of the horses. He snaked to the left.

"This all would have been so simple if you and your husband had done as I told you," Killibrew grumbled. "As much gold as you're rumored to have, you can spare a few saddlebags full."

"For what you have done you will reap a different harvest," Winona said flatly.

Killibrew leaned back. "You talk real poetical. But you must not care for those brats as much as you let on, or you wouldn't have come after us. Or did you think I strung up that likeness of your youngest daughter for the hell of it?"

"Youngest? Melissa Braddock isn't mine. Only Evelyn."

Ezriah didn't understand why Killibrew swore a mean streak, then cackled inanely. He was crawling through a patch of parry primrose. Common along mountain waterways, primrose grew to a height of two feet and was noted for its five-petaled purple flowers that smelled like the business end of a skunk. He froze when the young kidnapper gazed past him toward the mountains. A flower brushed his nose and an irresistible urge to sneeze came over him, an urge he fought by pinching his nostrils together so hard, it hurt.

Kyle turned back to the mare.

"At Bent's Fort they weren't too clear on how many younguns you had," Killibrew was telling Winona. "St. Vrain said two, but the blacksmith thought you had three."

"Does it make a difference?" Winona asked.

"In the long run, no, but I don't like to tote unnecessary baggage." Killibrew sighed. "It's too bad you and your Injunlovin' husband didn't take me seriously. Now your entire family has to die, and the Braddock kid for good measure."

"You blame us for your own bloodthirsty nature?" Winona countered. "You never planned to let any of us live anyway. Witnesses can talk."

"True enough," Killibrew said. "And your husband has a lot of friends in these parts. Friends who might take it into their heads to get revenge."

Ezriah parted a primrose and wriggled toward a cluster of small boulders. Once there he had only another fifty feet to go. If Winona could keep Killibrew and Kyle occupied, he'd get the drop on them. Wouldn't that be a hoot? Saving her hide was bound to improve her opinion of him.

A narrow opening between the boulders was an ideal spot to await his chance. Ezriah extended an arm to slide through—and froze a second time. Something had moved at the bottom of the boulder on the right. Something long and sinuous and low to the ground. A second later the blunt head of a snake appeared, its vertical pupils fixed on him with startling intensity. A triangular head rose a few inches and a forked tongue licked out.

It was a rattler. A young one, but lethal just the same. More so, in the opinion of some mountain men, who claimed their venom was twice as potent.

Ezriah's skin dappled with goose bumps and he bit his lower lip in order not to cry out. The snake's tongue was inches from his fingers. One bite, one nip, and his life was forfeit. Normally, rattlers hunted at night. This one must have been sunning itself and been disturbed by his approach.

A prickly rash broke out on Ezriah's neck and face. The urge to itch was nigh overpowering, but he resisted. Any movement, however slight, would trigger an attack. His mouth went dry as the rattler slid nearer. The next dart of its tongue almost brushed his fingertip.

Ezriah gulped, and waited for the reptile to wander elsewhere. But all it did was lie there and stare, its damnable tongue flicking, flicking, flicking. The seconds stretched into minutes and the snake still didn't move.

Beads of sweat dotted Ezriah's brow. One trickled into his good eye and stung terribly. Blinking would help, but he was afraid to blink for fear of what the rattler would do. He was aware that Killibrew and Winona were talking, but their conversation was a gibberish drone in the background. His attention was on the serpent and nothing else.

When it became apparent the snake wasn't going to traipse off, Ezriah had a brainstorm. He slowly slid his other arm down his side to the hilt of his fancy sword. His palm was slick with perspiration, and he wiped it on his pants. Gripping the sword, he slid it from the scabbard. He had to avoid sudden movement. The best he could do was edge the hilt higher a fraction at a time, and that took forever.

The rattler lowered its head and lay in a beam of sunlight. Its tongue stopped flicking, its eyes closed halfway.

Ezriah was willing to swear on a stack of Bibles that the damn thing was taking a nap. He started to move his hand away from its face, but the snake's black tongue darted out. *Damn you!* Ezriah railed. *Go find a plump mouse somewhere!*

The itching worsened, abetted by the hot sun burning down on Ezriah's back. He slid the sword out farther, tensing when the blade scraped on the scabbard. The viper lay still, soaking up the heat like a sponge, enjoying the rattlesnake equivalent of bliss.

A voice raised in anger intruded on Ezriah's concentration. Killibrew was mad as a wet rooster.

". . . get on your high horse and lecture me! I am what I am, and I make no bones about it. I'm no different than the Blackfeet or the Bloods. They've killed a heap more people than I ever will!"

"The Blackfeet and the Bloods kill whites who invade their territory," Winona said. "They do not kill for personal gain."

"Liar!" Killibrew declared. "I may not know a lot about Injuns, but I know that the more coup they count, the more they're looked up to by other Injuns. The more whites they kill, the greater they become. So don't tell me they don't kill for personal gain."

"But not out of greed," Winona clarified.

"You're splitting hairs," Killibrew accused her. "Nit-pickin' to justify the atrocities your kind commits! Atrocities no worse than what I aim to do to you and yours."

Ezriah had the sword three-quarters free. A little more would do it. But Killibrew's angry shouts had somehow agitated the rattler. Its tongue resumed flicking and its head rose a thimble's width above the ground.

Someone once told Ezriah that snakes didn't have ears; they heard with their tongues. Whether it was true or not he couldn't say, but it was a safe assumption that every second he stayed there, he tempted fate. Western rattlers were notoriously bad-tempered when stirred up. Sort of like women.

"Many men have tried to slay my husband," he heard Winona say. "Many graves are testimony to their foolishness."

"Spare me, squaw. I don't scare."

The rattler settled down to earth again and coiled backward, closer to the boulder. Not much, only a couple of inches, enough, though, that Ezriah could breathe a smidgen easier. He nearly had the sword out when the tip snagged on the end of the scabbard. Try as he might, he couldn't extend his arm far enough to draw the sword the rest of the way. Not at the angle he was lying. So, riveted to the reptile, he slowly twisted just enough for him to move his arm the necessary inch.

Rather than chop at the snake and raise a commotion, Ezriah elected to stab it. A single clean stroke should do the job. Reversing his grip, he brought the curved steel around in front of him. Not all the way. Enough so he could see tapered tip and gauge the proper angle to strike.

The snake's head was two, maybe two-and-a-half inches wide. Not the largest of targets. Ezriah focused on the flat part immediately behind its eyes. He would get only one chance. If he missed, the rattler would either retreat under the boulder or attack him in a frenzy.

Ezriah tried to swallow, but his mouth was too dry. Holding the sword securely, he bunched his shoulder muscles, prayed to heaven he didn't miss, and speared the sword at the serpent. Simultaneously, as if it had divined that its life was threatened, the rattler started to rise and opened its mouth wide, the retractable fangs near the front of its upper jaw swinging forward, both dripping venom.

The sword sheared into the upper portion of the snake's mouth, cleaved into the scaly flesh between its eyes, and sliced clean through its head, pinning it to the soil.

Ezriah had done it!

Erupting in its death throes, the rattler whipped its body from side to side. Its tail, until that moment silent, lashed wildly, buzzing like a swarm of hornets. In an effort to quiet it, Ezriah grabbed the thick body midway back. He felt the snake ripple to his touch and recoiled in instinctive loathing. The tail buzzed louder. Frantic, he lunged over the pinned head and gripped the snake's hard, segmented rattles. It muffled the noise, but again, the feel of the vibrating segments against his skin spooked him, and he let go. As he drew back, he saw the viper shake itself, and the head started to slide up the sword toward him. Terrified of being nicked by those deadly fangs, Ezriah rolled to the left, out of harm's way.

The rattler gave a last convulsive quake and died.

Ezriah shuddered at his close call and went to yank his sword out. A shadow fell across him. Glancing up, he looked into the grinning face of the youngest cutthroat and the muzzle of a rifle.

"It's not your day, is it, old-timer?"

Chapter Eleven

Nate King drew rein and studied the terrain ahead. Something was wrong. The instincts he had honed over decades of living in the wild warned him that the forest held danger. He searched for the source but saw nothing to account for his unease. Starting to lift the reins to move on, he noticed the bay's ears were pricked. It, too, knew something or someone was out there. Animal or man, that was the question.

Ordinarily, Nate would circle wide and go on his way unmolested. On several occasions he had outwitted hostile war parties lying in ambush by just such a tactic. But now he had the girls to think of.

Nate was fairly certain it was Bittner and Haro who were waiting for him. There had been no sign of Indians, and it was too early yet for mountain lions and grizzlies to be abroad. How had they spotted him before he spotted them? The obvious answer was the Pawnee. He frowned, annoyed at his carelessness. It had cost him the element of surprise and now might cost his life. To say nothing of the fate in store for the girls.

Nate could go around as he originally intended. But that might anger Bittner and his companion, and there was no telling what they might do to Evelyn and Melissa. Acting in the belief the kidnappers wouldn't kill him before they got their hands on the gold, he took a calculated risk.

Placing the Hawken across his legs, Nate nudged the bay into a walk through a mix of peachleaf willows and oaks. The woods were as still as a graveyard; no birds chirped, no squirrels chattered, even the usually noisy chipmunks were in hiding. It was as if all the animals were holding their collective breath waiting for the next step in the eternal tableau of fang and claw to unfold.

A clearing appeared, and for a moment Nate couldn't credit his eyes. Standing alone in the center was Evelyn. In his joy at finding her and his eagerness to take her into his arms he went to spur the bay, and just as quickly relaxed his legs. Whangs torn from a buckskin shirt had been tied around her ankles, and her cheeks glistened with tears. Her mouth was moving, but no sounds were coming out. He watched her lips and saw that she was mouthing the words "Go back, Pa! Go back!" over and over.

Nate kneed the bay on, and Evelyn stiffened. Evidently she'd assumed he didn't realize he was riding into a trap, and from her lungs exploded a cry of anguish.

"Get out of here, Pa! Run! They're waiting for you!"

At that, a rough-hewn giant bounded from the undergrowth and pointed a rifle at her head. "One wrong move, mister, and your girl is wolf bait!"

Nate reined up.

"I'm not bluffing!" the man shouted. It had to be Bittner. His bulbous nose and unkempt beard fit the description. "The 'breed has his rifle fixed on your precious brat too! Even if you shoot me, he'll shoot her!"

Nate had figured as much. It was the only reason he hadn't dropped Bittner in his tracks the second the giant showed himself. "Don't harm her!" he called out. "I'll do whatever you want. I'm a reasonable man." He wanted to give the impression that he was cowed with fear for his daughter's welfare, that he would lick Bittner's boots if he had to.

Bittner laughed. "Hell, I'm a reasonable man myself." He beckoned. "Come and join us, why don't you? Hold that long gun out to one side and don't touch your pistols, not if you want the fruit of your loins to go on breathing."

His eyes on Evelyn, Nate did as he was commanded. He looked at her with all the love and devotion brimming in his heart every father felt for every daughter, and he was rewarded with a tiny smile. Despite her despair, she returned his gaze with the trusting stare of one who had unbounded faith in his judgment and his ability. He would not disappoint her.

Bittner moved to the left, grinning wolfishly, immensely pleased with himself. "This was a lot easier than I reckoned it would be. The mighty Nate King. The great Grizzly Killer, as the redskins call you. Hell, your reputation is all hot air if you ask me."

From the vegetation across the clearing stepped Haro. He had Melissa by the shoulder and pushed her toward the center. His rifle rose to cover Nate, his flat, cold eyes those of someone who could kill without a qualm. Men, women, children—it made no difference to him. He was the deadlier of the pair by far.

Nate smiled, and Haro blinked in surprise.

"Drop the Hawken," Bittner directed, and when the rifle thudded to the grass, he warily sidestepped the bay and picked it up. Laughing anew, he nodded at Nate's waist. "Now the belly armory. One at a time. Use two fingers."

Once again Nate meekly followed the gruff instructions to the letter. His knife was next. "Can I climb down now?" he asked politely.

Bittner had kicked the pistols well out of reach, and he did likewise with the Bowie. "Sure. Feel free." He couldn't seem to stop laughing. "A family reunion is in order."

Holding his hands out from his sides, Nate swung his left leg clear of its stirrup, swiveled in the saddle, and slid off. Haro was glued to him like a hawk to prey, the muzzle of the 'breed's rifle moving as he moved. He walked to Evelyn, hunkered, and tugged at the whangs binding her ankles. She stood stock-still until he was done, then threw her arms around him and buried her wet face in the hollow of his neck.

"Oh, pa," Evelyn breathed. "I'm sorry. So, so sorry."

Nate had to cough to lessen a constriction in his throat before he could respond. "Sorry about what?"

"They'd never have caught you if they didn't have me. It's my fault." Evelyn sobbed softly.

Hugging her close, Nate stroked her head. "That's like a beaver blaming the castoreum for luring it into the jaws of a trap when we both know the trapper is to blame." He pecked her hair. "No, little one. The only ones at fault here are the men who stole you. And they will pay for what they have done."

"How touching." Bittner reeked of sarcasm. "But what kind of father are you? You shouldn't make promises you can't keep."

Nate saw Melissa staring forlornly at him, saw the tears in her eyes, and gestured. Haro released her, and she ran to him and threw her tiny arms around his neck and commenced crying.

Bittner sidled toward the warrior, his teeth showing through his beard, and poked Haro with an elbow. "Look at him! And you were worried he'd put up a fight. Hell, my granny is tougher than this so-called Grizzly Killer."

"We should kill him," Haro said. "We should kill all of them."

Nate wrapped his right arm around both the girls and placed his right hand close to the hem of his buckskin shirt.

"God, you're a bloodthirsty devil," Bittner criticized the 'breed. "But you're not too bright. If we kill him, we'll never get the gold. It's best we take him to Killibrew and let shorty decide what to do."

"It is a mistake not to kill him," Haro said somberly. "This one has the eyes of a cornered wolf. Look at him. See for yourself."

Bittner glanced at Nate and chuckled. "All I see is a man scared to death we'll harm the girls if he breathes wrong. We have him over a barrel. He's helpless." Bittner paused. "But if it will make you feel more at ease, tie his wrists."

Haro did just that. He had Nate stand and hold both arms straight out, then used the whangs that had bound Evelyn's ankles to bind Nate's wrists. He tied the buckskin strips tightly, knotting them several times.

Evelyn and Melissa clung to Nate's legs. Evelyn stopped weeping, but Melissa was a fountain of misery.

While Haro covered them, Bittner gathered up Nate's weapons, wrapped them in Nate's own bedroll, and retied the bedroll behind Nate's saddle. He hiked a foot to mount, then lowered it again. "No. We'll make better time if the brats ride. Their small legs slow us down too much." He pried Melissa off and hoisted her up.

Evelyn was next. As the giant swung her up in front of the younger girl, Evelyn never took her eyes off Nate.

"Remember, girl," Bittner said. "Try to light a shuck and we'll blow a hole in your pa you can put your fist through."

Offended, Evelyn snapped, "What do you take me for? I would never run out on my own father."

Bittner looked at Nate. "That's some kid you've got there, King. Damned near gave us the slip, and Haro can track with the best of 'em."

Nate patted Evelyn's knee. "She's some girl, all right," he said, and she gave his hand a tender squeeze.

"Walk on ahead," Bittner directed, grasping the bay's reins. "Head northeast until you cut Buzzard Creek and follow it east. Killibrew should be camped next to it, waiting for us."

Haro hadn't lowered his rifle once. Instead of following, he angled to the right and hiked abreast of Nate, as alert as a cougar stalking a buck. He was taking no chances.

Nate hooked his thumbs in his leather belt. In another half an hour it would be dark. That was when he would make his move. Or shortly after. He intentionally ignored Haro to try and lull the 'breed off guard.

Bittner whistled happily for a while, then cleared his throat. "One thing puzzles me, mister. You say you love your girl. Yet you saw that effigy. Didn't you give a damn we might kill her?"

"I was counting on your greed to keep her alive," Nate said. To elaborate would be pointless. A rogue like Bittner could never comprehend the abiding affection of a parent for a child. Only another parent could.

"Gambling with your brat's life sounds like mighty high stakes to me," Bittner said. "I guess it shows how much Killibrew knows. He swore to me you'd be clay in our hands."

"There's no predicting what people will do sometimes," Nate remarked.

"Ain't that the truth. I remember this dove down to New Orleans. I bought her a new dress, bought her some flowers from a street vendor, took her out to dinner at the best tavern I could afford, and what did she do? She wouldn't come up to my room later. Claimed she had a headache." Bittner swore. "I wasted enough drinking money on her to keep me in booze for a month."

Nate glimpsed a flash of blue off among the trees. Buzzard Creek, unless he was mistaken. So named from the time a couple of trappers found nine dead vultures in a pool low down in the foothills. All nine had been charred to a crisp, feathers and all, and some looked as if they had been blown apart from the inside out. No one at rendezvous knew what to make of it until someone suggested the vultures had sought shelter from a thunderstorm in a high tree and been struck by lightning. Ever after, the creek was known as Buzzard Creek.

Bittner was in a talkative mood. "Tell me something, King. How is it the Indians hereabouts are so friendly to you they showed you where to find all those nuggets? What makes you so special?"

"I don't hate them for the color of their skin."

"There has to be more to it than that. And it can't just be because you took a Shoshone squaw, neither. The Crows and Utes aren't on friendly terms with the Shoshones, but they think as highly of you as her own people. What's your secret?"

"All I do is I treat them the same as I would anyone else. That includes half-breeds." Nate glanced at Haro.

Bittner still wasn't convinced. "There has to be more, I tell you. I've known coons who were as peaceable as the year is long and wouldn't harm a hair on a Blackfoot's head, yet most Indians wouldn't give them the time of day."

"Treat a person with respect and nine times out of ten they'll return the favor," Nate said. That, and a lot of luck, accounted for his wide acceptance. Shortly after his arrival in the mountains he had stumbled on an old Crow in need of help, and the Crows had never forgotten. The Utes had tried to wipe his family out until he arranged a truce with another tribe on their behalf. The Cheyennes left him alone because of his friendship with one of their leaders. And so it went.

"You're a strange one, mister," Bittner commented. "Most whites think the only good Indian is a dead one. The more of us push west, the more the savages will resent it. Eventually we'll do to them as we did to those back east."

Nate hated to admit it, but the cutthroat might be right. Each year more and more whites moved west. Most were bound for California or Oregon, but it wouldn't be long—

in his lifetime perhaps—before towns and cities sprouted on the plains and in the mountains. The incursion was bound to upset many of the tribes, and who could blame them? They had dwelled there since time immemorial. The result would be bloodshed on a wide scale, exactly as occurred in the original thirteen colonies when the tribes there were displaced. And later, when the whites spread between the Appalachians and the Mississippi River.

Nate's mentor and best friend, Shakespeare McNair, was of the opinion that one day the wilderness would run scarlet with blood, that the past warfare east of the Mississippi would pale in comparison to the slaughter west of it. Nate prayed to God his friend was wrong, but Shakespeare rarely was.

Should that long-dreaded day take place, Nate would have a fateful choice to make: Should he side with his own kind or his adopted people? It would be the hardest decision of his life. He could only hope the Shoshones continued in their peaceful ways and didn't take up arms against the invaders.

The babble of rapidly flowing water over jagged rocks reached Nate's ears. He threaded through a final uneven row of cottonwoods and stood on the bank of Buzzard Creek. Several small fish darted from shore, and on the other side a rabbit bounded into the brush. He stepped to the bay and reached for Evelyn.

"What the hell do you think you're doing?" This from Bittner, who leveled his rifle.

"It's been a hot day. The girls could use a drink."

Bittner gestured for him to move back. "I decide when we'll stop. They'll drink when I say so and not before. Keep moving."

Nate gave his daughter a look that said "I'm sorry," and headed east. Haro was still off to his right but had fallen a few steps behind. He could slip his hand up under his shirt whenever the time was right.

Out of the blue Bittner asked, "What if we made a deal with you, King? What if we agreed to let the brats go in exchange for your word that you'd guide us to the stream where you found the gold?"

"I'm supposed to trust you?" Nate would sooner trust a Comanche not to slit his throat or a hungry silvertip not to eat him.

"We'll let you watch them ride off," Bittner proposed. "The four of us won't leave your side, and once they're gone you can honor your end of the bargain. How much fairer can we be?"

"Would Killibrew agree to the idea?"

"I'm positive I can persuade him to go along. The girls were a means to an end, nothing more. All we've ever really wanted is the gold."

"I'll think it over," Nate stalled. He had his own plan for resolving the situation.

To the west, the golden orb of the sun perched on far purple peaks. The shadows lengthened and a brisk breeze rustled the leaves, a harbinger of oncoming twilight. As casually as he could, Nate slid his right hand across his belt to his right hip and reassured himself the telltale bulge was still there.

Haro and Bittner were in for an unwelcome surprise. Unbeknownst to them, on Nate's last trip to Bent's Fort he had made a frivolous purchase. Frivolous in that he'd bought something he didn't need and might never have a use for, but something that might come in handy in a fix.

The dull clomp of the bay's hoofs beat in steady cadence. A third of the sun was devoured by the mountains, and the temperature fell a few degrees. Nate glanced over a shoulder every now and then, ostensibly at the girls but actually to mark its descent. He had to be utmostly careful, what with Haro studying his every movement, his every expression.

Nate wasn't the only one with finely honed instincts. The 'breed suspected he would try something but had no inkling what or when. That gave him a slight edge.

In contrast, Bittner's gold fever had rendered him as dull as a blunt blade. "Try to put yourself in our boots, King. The most money I ever had at any one time was thirty-five dollars and sixty-four cents. I recollect it so well because I thought I could live high on the hog for months, but it only lasted two weeks." He swore, and muttered, "Who'd have thought that other fella had a full house?"

Nate smiled at Evelyn and Melissa. The sun was half gone.

"Just once I'd like to get ahead," Bittner rambled on. "Just once I'd like to sleep in silk sheets and have servants wait on me hand and foot. Just once I'd like to feel as if I was somebody important."

"You can't measure a man's worth by how much money he has," Nate mentioned, and was laughed to scorn.

"What rock have you been living under? Money is power. Money is respect. Money is everything. Those who have it are a whole hell of a lot better off than those who don't."

"The Good Book says money is the root of all evil."

"So you're a Bible-thumper? Who'd have thought it. I've got nothing against it personally, but if I was to live by the Golden Rule, as my ma always wanted us to do, I'd have been planted six feet under ages ago." Bittner paused. "Turning the other cheek is a surefire invite to an early grave."

"Maybe one day it won't be," Nate said, looking back. Two-thirds of the sun had been swallowed. It wouldn't be long.

Haro unexpectedly halted. "We kill Grizzly Killer," he announced. "We kill him now." Just like that, he sighted down his rifle, his forefinger curling around the trigger.

"Hold on there, damn it!" Bittner dropped the reins and darted between them. "What the hell has gotten into you? How many times must I tell you we need him alive to find the damn gold?"

"I do not care about the yellow metal anymore," Haro said. "I care about my life."

"He's unarmed, for God's sake," Bittner said irritably. "What's he going to do? Bite you to death? With you holding a gun on him?" He shook a brawny fist. "Get ahold of yourself or there will be hell to pay."

Haro slowly lowered the rifle. "He plans to kill us. I can feel it."

"Of course he does," Bittner said. "He doesn't want us to hurt the brats. But if we can talk him into agreeing to my little arrangement, no one has to kill anybody."

An orange crescent crowned the western peaks. It would be another few minutes yet until the sun sank entirely, but Nate couldn't pass up the opportunity. Bittner's back was to him and Haro was looking at Bittner. Standing sideways so they couldn't see his right hand, Nate worked it underneath his shirt, up under his belt.

The brainchild of a man named Henry Deringer, derringers were all the rage. Gamblers used them as hideouts for when their integrity was challenged. Travelers carried them in their jacket pockets for protection. Women carried them in their handbags. Frontiersmen relied on them as reserve weapons when their rifles and pistols were spent.

Fitted with the latest percussion system, and sold with a tin of percussion caps, derringers had the distinction of rarely misfiring. Their one drawback was their limited range. Large derringers were effective up to ten paces at most. For a small derringer like Nate's, the range was cut in half. His was the smallest made, a single-shot .41-caliber model. As was typical, a flowery design was etched on the silver lock plate, the lower portion of the hammer, and the silver trigger guard, adding a touch of artistic elegance to the lethal little man-stopper.

Holding it next to his leg, Nate thumbed back the hammer and stepped behind Bittner. He would rather shoot Haro, but the 'breed would see him if he moved to either side to fire. Since he couldn't kill them both with one shot, he had to kill the one he could.

Nate was raising the derringer when a question popped into his head: *Why couldn't I shoot them both with one bullet?* It was feasible. If he placed the slug just right, it would pass completely through Bittner and strike the 'breed. He pointed the derringer at the back of the giant's bull neck, to the left of the spine. The human neck is one of the softest, most vulnerable spots on the body, and a ruptured jugular can kill a man within seconds.

"Leave King to me," Bittner told Haro. "I know what I'm doing."

Nate squeezed the trigger.

At the loud *crack,* a crimson geyser sprayed from the front of the giant's neck, splattering Haro. Bittner stiffened and grabbed at his throat. Haro jerked backward as if struck, and pivoting with lightning speed, he melted into the greenery in the blink of an eye.

Without a second to lose, Nate turned toward the bay, toward the bedroll and his guns. He had taken two strides when a blood-caked hand closed on his shoulder and he was spun around.

Bittner's throat was a ravaged ruin. He had dropped his rifle, and now, growling deep in his chest, he clamped his thick fingers onto Nate's neck. "Bastard!" he roared, blood spurting from the jagged hole and from the corners of his mouth. Digging his fingers into Nate's flesh, he squeezed with all the power in his bulging sinews.

Nate grabbed the bigger man's wrists and sought to wrench loose, but Bittner was not to be denied. Nate twisted to the right, twisted to the left, and the other man clung on, his hard-as-iron fingers digging deeper, ever deeper. Staggering back, Nate struck Bittner with his fists. His blows would have crumpled lesser men, but the giant was as impervious as chain mail.

"Die!" Bittner raged, and more blood gushed. His beard was soaked, his shirt stained red.

"Pa!" Evelyn screamed. "Look out! The trees!"

Nate glanced to his left and saw Haro in the shadows, taking deliberate aim. Instantly, he swung to the right, swinging Bittner into the line of fire at the exact split second Haro's rifle spat lead and smoke. Bittner's forehead exploded, and gore showered onto Nate's face and chest. Bittner's fingers went limp. So did Bittner. Deprived of the spark of life, the man who had yearned to be rich at any cost swayed like a steer bled for slaughter, and fell.

Spinning, Nate ran to the bay. In a twinkling he had Evelyn in one arm and Melissa in the other and was hurtling toward the woods. A pistol cracked, and a stinging sensation spiked his left shoulder. Foliage closed around them as Haro's second pistol banged. A slug thumped into a cottonwood and slivers peppered his cheek.

"Run and don't look back!" Nate commanded. Lowering them, he gave the girls a push. Then, rotating, he did the last thing Haro would expect: He sped back into the open, making for the bay again.

The sight of Bittner's rifle in the grass caused Nate to veer toward it instead. It wasn't wrapped in a blanket, and was ready for use. He took a long stride and leaped, his arms outflung.

Out of the growth charged Haro, a gleaming knife held aloft. Nate's fingers found the rifle as Haro reached him. Tempered steel cleaved the air, the blade missing Nate by a hair and glancing off the rifle he was trying to level. Nate flung himself to the rear to gain room to move, but Haro was on him like a cougar on a marmot. The knife slashed at his neck, at his face, at his stomach.

A rut in the ground proved Nate's downfall. He tripped and fell onto his back. Above him reared the 'breed, triumph lighting Haro's dark eyes, the blade poised to kill. They both knew Nate couldn't stop it from descending.

They both knew Haro had won. So it was difficult to say which of them was more surprised by the shot that rang loud and clear—and the third nostril Haro acquired. The 'breed staggered, shifted partway around, and melted to the ground, the knife that had almost claimed Nate's life sinking into the soil beside him.

Nate rose onto his elbows.

Evelyn stood next to Bittner's body, one of the big man's pistols clutched in her small hands. "I couldn't let him kill you, Pa," she said softly. "I just couldn't."

Chapter Twelve

Winona King was as surprised as Killibrew when Kyle marched Ezriah Hampton to the campfire at gunpoint. Ezriah gave her an apologetic look and bowed his head in shame at being caught.

"Look at what I found," Kyle said.

Killibrew jumped up. "What the hell is this? Are they fallin' out of the sky?" Poking Ezriah in the chest, he rasped, "You weren't much of a messenger, old man! The idea was for the Kings to fetch us their gold, not dog our steps to the Missouri. Didn't you make it plain what we would do to the sprouts?"

"I did exactly as you told me," Ezriah said, "but they couldn't abide the thought of a filthy animal like you so much as touching the girls."

Flushing with anger, Killibrew balled a fist and punched the old trapper in the stomach. Ezriah doubled over, sputtering in agony, and pitched onto his hands and knees. Still not satisfied, Killibrew drew back a boot and kicked him in the ribs, pitching Ezriah onto his side where he thrashed in torment.

"That's just a taste of what's in store for the aggravation you've caused me, you bastard," Killibrew declared. He drew back his foot to kick Hampton a second time.

"Leave him alone!" Winona cried. Springing in front of Hampton, she shielded him with her body. As much as she detested him, he *had* gone after the girls on his own to atone for letting them be taken in the first place. And Killibrew's earlier comment about how Ezriah had been ready to throw his life away to try and save Evelyn and Melissa had made her realize the depth of his affection for them. Perhaps the old man wasn't as despicable as she'd led herself to believe.

Denied one outlet for his wrath, Killibrew chose another. Grabbing Winona by the front of her dress, he shook her until her teeth rattled, then thrust a foot behind her and shoved her to the ground beside Hampton. "Don't butt in again, bitch!" he hissed. Hiking his rifle, he took a step, about to bash her over the head with the heavy stock.

Kyle suddenly flung out a hand. "Think about what you're doing! If we hurt her, her husband won't like it much. And we need him to get the gold, don't we?"

Killibrew turned to stone. His fury slowly subsided and was replaced by an icy, more menacing, expression. Stepping back, he lowered his arms. "What to do? What to do?" he said thoughtfully. "It seems to me drastic measures are called for."

"How drastic?" Kyle asked.

Winona slid to Ezriah. He was curled into a ball and breathing raggedly. "How bad is it?"

"The polecat about staved in my rib cage," Ezriah grunted, "but I'm as tough as jerky. I'll live." He mustered a grin.

Killibrew commenced to pace back and forth in an excess of violent energy. "We have to face facts. Nate King has no intention of giving us what we want. Why? Because he

152

hasn't taken us serious. None of them have. So it's time we set them straight."

Kyle glanced at Winona. "You're not fixing to harm the woman, are you?"

Killibrew stopped dead. "She's a *squaw*, boy. A lousy Injun. Sure, she's female, but so is a heifer, and you wouldn't object if I carved up a cow, would you?"

"I don't like the idea of harming women."

"You're beginnin' to annoy me," Killibrew said. "Why don't you take the old geezer for a walk, if it bothers you that much. You'll have to go a ways. She might scream. They usually do."

The younger man stayed where he was. "When you asked me to join up, you swore to me no one would be hurt. You said you had it all planned out. You said King wouldn't dare give us trouble. You said a lot of things that turned out not to be true."

"How was I to know the whole damn family has grit up to their ears?" Killibrew responded. "Any sensible person would have given in. But these Kings are as pesky as wolverines. They don't do what you expect."

"So why go on with it?" Kyle said.

"What else would you have us do?" Killibrew impatiently rejoined. "Give up and head for St. Louis?"

"Why not?" Kyle asked. "They've called our bluff. We should fold our cards and walk away from the table. Ride on out and make ourselves scarce while we still can."

"You're serious?"

"We haven't killed anyone yet. The worst anyone can claim is that we took the girls for a couple of days. We can say we found them wandering in the woods. It'll be their word against ours. And since the girls haven't been laid a hand on, we'll be set free."

Killibrew stopped pacing and faced him. "You've got it all worked out, haven't you, lunkhead? But you're forgettin' the most important part. The *gold*. I'm not leavin' until I get it. And no matter what I have to do, I *will* get it. One way or another."

Winona stood and tried to help Ezriah to stand. She was grateful the younger man was standing up for them, but she feared he had sorely misjudged the leader. Killibrew was on the verge of losing his temper again, and if the young one wasn't careful, he would suffer the brunt of Killibrew's wrath.

"Just so you don't harm the woman or the kids," Kyle said.

Winona waited for the explosion sure to follow, but Killibrew smiled as if he thought it was humorous and started to turn toward the fire. She never saw him grip one of his pistols. He was too clever. The next moment he spun, his arm out, the pistol cocked, and at near point-blank range he discharged the heavy-caliber flintlock into Kyle's temple.

The younger man was propelled backward. Arms pinwheeling, he staggered to a stop, gaped at his killer, then collapsed like a puppet with its strings cut. A sizable chunk of the back of his skull had been blown away, and his brains began to seep onto the grass.

Maniacal rage seized Killibrew. Stomping to the corpse, he kicked it again and again and again, an excess of brutal savagery that didn't end until Kyle's face resembled a pulped melon. Whirling, Killibrew shoved the pistol under his belt and trained his rifle on Winona and Ezriah. "Now that the Good Samaritan has been dealt with, let's get on with it, shall we?"

Ezriah couldn't straighten, but that didn't stop him from shuffling in front of Winona and saying, "You'll have to go through me to get to her."

"Easily done," Killibrew said. A quick lunge, and he rammed the barrel of his rifle into Hampton's midsection. As the old man folded, Killibrew swung the stock in a high arc that caught him on the head.

Ezriah buckled, groaned, and was still.

154

Winona leaped at Killibrew, but he had the reflexes of a cat. Spinning, he aimed the rifle at her chest, halting her in midstride.

"Don't even think it, squaw. I've had my fill. I'd as soon shoot you as spit on you." Killibrew sidestepped to the left. "Sit by the fire a spell. I have preparations to make."

Acutely conscious that at any instant his gun might spew searing death, Winona curled her legs under her. She wanted to help Hampton. His hat had fallen off, and a gash below his hairline was pouring scarlet. His weapons, including his sword, were a dozen feet past him, where Kyle had dumped them. She considered making a bid for them, but Killibrew was watching her intently as he moved about the clearing.

Winona was sorry Kyle had died in her defense, but he had brought it on himself by hooking up with his slayer. Some men—and some women—were vicious by nature. They delighted in inflicting suffering and in taking lives, and no amount of talk could change their sadistic ways.

The Shoshones believed a proper upbringing forged proper character, but it would be wasted on a person with Killibrew's temperament. He was what her husband called a "bad seed," someone born with a wicked streak ingrained into their being.

Winona and Nate once got into a long and involved discussion about whether white men or red men were more violent. She had been of the opinion whites were; they routinely indulged in robbery and murder, as Nate conceded, and in some of the cities back east it wasn't safe to be abroad in certain quarters after the sun went down. In contrast, among her people thievery and murder were virtually unknown.

Nate had argued convincingly that she was being unfair. True, Shoshones seldom slew members of their own tribe, but like other warrior societies they regularly sent war parties against their enemies and killed as many as they could.

Warfare was their way of life, and the torture of captives much too common. Proof that when all was said and done, the two races weren't that much different.

Killibrew had bent over a saddle. When he straightened he held a coiled rope. He scanned the trees ringing the camp and became interested in a stately oak all by itself on the bank of Buzzard Creek. "That will do right fine," he announced, and motioned. "Mosey on over here, woman."

Winona moved slowly, buying time. She had some notion of what he had in mind, but with his rifle centered on her sternum, to resist invited the same fate as Kyle's.

"Stand with your back to the trunk," Killibrew directed, "and place your hands behind it."

Once her hands were tied Winona would be helpless, utterly at the mercy of a two-legged fiend. "I would rather die fighting," she said.

Killibrew nodded as if he had expected her to refuse. Shifting, he pointed his rifle at the crumpled form of Ezriah Hampton. "Maybe you don't care about your own hide, but how about his? Either you do as I tell you or I'll finish him off."

Winona hesitated. Part of her felt she didn't owe Hampton a thing; she still blamed him for the whole mess, to a degree. The other part of her had been touched by how he had rallied to her defense. She glanced at him, at the blood caking the lower half of his face and the ridge of scar tissue over his left eye, and she was lost. "I will do as you want." Gritting her teeth at her stupidity, she leaned back against the oak and extended her arms behind her.

Snickering, Killibrew drew his ivory-hilted dagger, cut a three-foot length of the rope, and sidled around the trunk.

Seconds later a loop encircled Winona's left wrist. She almost changed her mind, almost pulled away, but then another loop was applied to her right wrist and she was yanked backward, slamming her spine against the bole. Killibrew had her right where he wanted her. Pain seared her wrists, as the rope was tied much too tightly.

Giving a final tug to ensure the rope was secure, Killibrew crowed, "This should do just fine. Now we can get down to business."

Winona girded herself for the horror to come. She thought of Nate. She thought of her son and her daughter, and she smiled.

Killibrew nonchalantly walked around the oak, his rifle resting across his shoulder. He had all the time in the world now. "What do you have to be so consarned happy about?" he asked.

"I have lived a full life. A good life," Winona said.

"So you're ready to give up the ghost? Is that it?" Killibrew set his rifle on the ground and again drew his dagger. "You won't die for a good, long while yet. I'm going to whittle on you some, enough to hear you scream. Enough to have you beg me to stop."

Winona wished he were closer so she could spit in his face. "That will never happen," she vowed.

Killibrew held the dagger so the sun glinted off the blade. "I've carved up a few people in my time, lady. Before I was done, each and every one blubbered like a baby. You won't be any different." His moon face glistened with anticipation, and he stepped up close.

Winona had been waiting for just that moment. She drove her right foot at his groin, but he nimbly sidestepped. The dagger flashed twice in swift succession. Sharp pangs seared her, and as she lowered her leg she saw two slashes in her buckskin dress, one low on her shin, the other high on her thigh. The cuts weren't deep, but they were painful.

"Try that again and I'll hamstring you," Killibrew said. He raised his dagger so she could see her blood on the blade.

"Do you honestly expect me to do nothing while you torture me?" Winona responded. She would fight him to her dying breath.

"Unless you want me to walk over and slit the old man's throat, that's exactly what you'll do." Killibrew ran a finger along his dagger, then flicked the finger at her face, spattering her with red drops. "We want you lookin' pretty when that Injun-lovin' man of yours arrives."

"Nate?" Winona envisioned him in her mind's eye, approaching cautiously until he saw her tied to the tree, bent and bloody. He would charge in heedless of the danger, right into Killibrew's gun sights.

"Got another husband I don't know about?" Killibrew said, and laughed. Leaning toward her, he propped his left hand against the oak and lightly tapped the tip of his dagger on her chin. "I have to admit I don't understand men like him. I mean, I can savvy a man who diddles a squaw for the fun of it. But to marry one? To take an Injun woman for better or for worse till death do you part? Why the hell would he want to tie himself down like that?"

"It could be he loves me," Winona said.

"Love an Injun? That's the part that puzzles me the most." Killibrew looked her up and down. "What is there about you heathens to love?"

"More than someone like you could ever appreciate."

"Is that so?" Killibrew said. His dagger flashed, opening her right cheek from her ear to her chin.

Winona winced at the burning torment and felt the lower half of her cheek grow moist. Again she had the impression he had cut just deep enough to draw blood but not deep enough to mutilate or kill. He was toying with her to prolong her suffering. Blood dribbled into the corner of her mouth and she tasted its salty tang.

"I wonder if he'll still love you when I get through?" Killibrew said. "You won't be nearly as good-lookin'. Not unless he's partial to females without noses and ears." He pressed the dagger to the side of her nose and gave a light twist. "My, my. You sure do bleed nice."

Winona started to kick him but saw Hampton over by the fire, as helpless as a newborn babe. In frustration she stamped her foot and spat blood at their feet.

"If you have something to say, feel free," Killibrew said. "Might as well use your tongue while you still have it." Again his dagger licked out.

This time Winona's upper arm was the target, and this time he did cut deep. So deep she nearly cried out. Steeling herself against the inevitable, she closed her eyes so he wouldn't see the effect he was having.

"Now, now. I don't want you fallin' asleep on me." Killibrew pricked her side, and when that provoked no reaction, he jabbed the dagger into her shoulder. "Look at me when I'm carvin' you up like a Sunday grouse."

Winona rubbed her hands from side to side, seeking to loosen the rope enough to slip free. It gouged into her wrists, promising to scrape them raw if she didn't stop. But raw wrists were nothing compared to what the moon-faced killer had in store.

"I'll only tell you once," Killibrew said, and stabbed her in the hip.

Winona's eyes opened of their own accord, and she threw back her head to scream. The blade had bit to the bone. It was excruciating. She thought her leg would give way under her, but it didn't.

"Go ahead. Shriek your lungs out," Killibrew goaded. "I told you that you would."

The reminder saved Winona from weakening. Closing her mouth, she glared defiantly.

Killibrew straightened and positioned himself in front of her. "So which will it be first? Your nose? An ear? Your tongue?" Mulling what to do, he scrutinized her with renewed carnal interest. "I shouldn't be hasty, though, should I? It would be a shame to let a luscious body like yours go to waste."

"Cut me if you must, but not the other."

David Thompson

"You don't have a say in the matter," Killibrew said, and placed his left hand on her bosom. "My-oh-my. Are these breasts or watermelons?"

Killibrew cackled, and it was then, as his head was bent back and his gaze was to the sky, that Winona kneed him between the legs, slamming her knee up and in with all her strength. It connected solidly, and it was her turn to laugh as Killibrew tottered backward, his face as purple as a grape, his eyes half bulging from their sockets. "My-oh-my," she mimicked him. "Was that your manhood or a twig?"

Killibrew couldn't answer. Gasping and shuddering, he oozed to his knees and cupped himself. The dagger fell to the dirt at his side. Spittle running over his lower lip, he whined like a stricken dog and bent partway over.

"I will not be groped," Winona said. "I will not be abused." Sliding as low as the rope permitted, she tried to kick him in the face, but he was just out of her reach.

"Bitch!" Killibrew spat. "Filthy, rotten bitch!" He attempted to stand, but his legs wouldn't support him. "As soon as I can get to my feet, you're mine. Hear me? Mine to do with as I please!"

Winona rubbed her wrists harder. They throbbed with agony as she twisted them right and left. She wouldn't stop until she rubbed them down to the bone, if that was what it took. But it shouldn't take quite that long. They were slick with blood, and the loops were slowly loosening.

"God, how you'll suffer!" Killibrew snarled. "I'll show you some tricks I've learned. Tricks an Apache would envy."

Winona strained to her utmost. She had to free herself before he recovered or all was lost.

"This is what I get for going easy on you," Killibrew said. "For not gutting you the moment I caught you spyin' on us."

Another factor was working against Winona. Blood had been seeping down her neck, down her thigh, and down both legs. In time the loss would weaken her to where she couldn't lift a finger in her defense. Desperate, she rubbed, rubbed, rubbed.

Fueled by anger, Killibrew lurched upright and teetered a few steps. One hand over his private parts, he steadied himself. "I was content to let you live until your old man showed up, but now that's changed, squaw. Now he'll find your lifeless body."

"Cut me loose!" Winona challenged. "Give me a knife and I will fight you, woman to man."

The color was fading from Killibrew's face. His mouth curling in contempt, he bent and retrieved his dagger. "You'd like that, wouldn't you? For me to be stupid enough to accept? It ain't going to happen. You'll die like a trussed lamb, a fitting end for a heathen who acts so high and mighty."

Winona was perplexed when he shoved the dagger into its sheath and walked to the fire. *What is he up to?* she wondered.

Killibrew selected a slender branch from the pile of firewood, broke the branch in half, and carefully poked at the burning logs. Twice he had to draw back from the flames. Finally he succeeded in rolling a red-hot piece of wood from the fire's heart. It hissed and gave off smoke as he pressed the two sticks against it and slowly stood.

Winona's wrists throbbed, but the rope wasn't loose enough yet. She braced herself against the oak, intending to kick him when he came close enough, but he had learned from his mistakes.

Killibrew placed the coal down, moved to the right as if to go behind the tree and check the rope, then abruptly pivoted and slammed his fist into her abdomen.

Brilliant pinpoints of light flared before Winona's eyes. She slumped forward, bile pumping from her throat into her mouth.

"Hungry, bitch?"

Iron fingers fastened onto Winona's chin. Her head was pushed back and bent at a spine-cracking angle. Her mouth was forced open. Through a haze she glimpsed the burning piece of wood, grasped between the two halves of the branch, and terror speared through her. *Killibrew was going to force it down her throat!*

"I saw this done to an Arapaho once. He got drunk and slapped a white fella, so a bunch of his friends took him out and fed him five or six burning coals."

The heat seared Winona's lips. She jerked to the side, or sought to. Killibrew had her in an unbreakable vise.

"You should have heard that Arapaho scream. It was a sight to behold, how blood kept pourin' from his mouth and nose, and how his stomach swelled up like an over-heated water skin."

Winona's vision cleared. Killibrew's leering face was inches from hers. The coal was next to her open mouth. A shake of his arm, and it would slide down her throat. Her end was imminent. Then a miracle occurred. Killibrew stiffened, and the point of a sword sliced up out of the center of his chest. He looked down at himself in stunned amazement, let go of the branches, and turned.

Ezriah Hampton couldn't keep his grip on the hilt. Too weak to do more than shake a gnarled fist, he cried, "Get away from her, you miserable son of a bitch!"

Killibrew opened his mouth, but all that came out was blood. His movements wooden and methodical, he drew a pistol and raised it to fire. He would be dead soon, but he wasn't dying alone. The hammer clicked as he curled it back.

Without hesitation, Winona gripped the oak and swung her legs as high as she could. It was high enough. Her ankles wrapped around Killibrew's neck, and she wrenched as the pistol went off. The ball meant for Hampton whizzed off into the trees.

"Damn you!" Killibrew railed, and smashed the flintlock against her leg.

Exerting every sinew in her body, Winona squeezed her ankles together. Ezriah reached out to help, but he was still hurting and keeled to his knees. It was up to her now to finish it—her and her alone. Winona squeezed harder, her ankles digging into Killibrew's neck as the rope had dug into her wrists. She squeezed and squeezed, her legs as taut as bowstrings.

Killibrew fought dearly for his waning life. He hit her. He tore at her ankles. He gripped her feet and pried. In a crazed frenzy, he bent his head and sank his teeth into her right leg.

"Die!" Winona cried, whipping from side to side. Her shoulders, her back, her arms were on fire. Suddenly throwing her whole body to the left, she twisted her ankles sharply in the opposite direction.

At a loud *crack,* Killibrew went limp. The flintlock fell from fingers sapped of vitality, and his legs gave way.

His weight was too much for Winona to bear. Her ankles parted, and Killibrew toppled with a thump, landing beside Ezriah. The old man roused and squinted up at her, grinning through the blood and the pulped flesh.

"For a female you're downright feisty."

At that, he passed out.

Three hours later, Nate King galloped out of the darkness into the clearing beside Buzzard Creek and drew rein. In front of him, his arm around her waist, sat Melissa. Behind him, her fingers hooked in his belt, was Evelyn. Nate saw two bodies stretched side by side under an oak tree, covered by blankets. Beside the fire, laughing and joking, were the love of his life and Ezriah Hampton.

"Ma!" Evelyn screeched, and she was off the lathered bay in a streak.

Mother and daughter ran to each other and embraced as Nate lowered a drowsy Melissa, then slid off himself.

Winona's dress was ripped and stained dark in spots and she was extremely pale, but otherwise she appeared to be all right. She came to him, and hugged him, and whispered in his ear, "My heart sings with joy, husband. I love you so, and always will."

Nate kissed her, speechless with elation. Evelyn clung to the both of them, sobbing for joy, and was joined by Melissa.

Ezriah Hampton hobbled over, chuckling to himself. The old-timer looked as if he had been stomped by a bull buffalo, but he was in exceptional spirits.

"Happy to see us?" Nate asked.

Ezriah glanced at Winona. "Do you want to spring the surprise, sugarplum, or should I do the honors?"

"Sugarplum?" Nate smiled at his wife. "Did he get his hands on some whiskey again?"

"Ezriah has changed his mind about returning to civilization so soon," Winona revealed. "He would rather live in the mountains awhile yet."

"And he'll need our help building a cabin," Nate guessed. "I understand."

Ezriah tittered. "Not quite, you don't. You see, I already have a place to live. For as long as I want." He winked at Winona. "Ain't that right?"

Nate King looked from one to the other, and as the truth sank in, he reached up and pinched himself. As luck would have it, he was wide awake.

Melissa Braddock's uncle did take her to North Carolina and raised her as if she were his own. She grew to be an independent, strong-willed young woman. At the outbreak of the Civil War she was working as a nurse, and it was while ministering to the wounded in an army hospital that she met Captain Jedidiah Lee, no relation to the great gen-

eral, and fell in love. Their marriage lasted forty-nine years. It was Captain Lee who included her reminiscences on her ordeal in the Rockies in his private journal, which formed the basis for this book.

WILDERNESS

#24

Mountain Madness

←————————————→

David Thompson

When Nate King comes upon a pair of green would-be trappers from New York, he is only too glad to risk his life to save them from a Piegan war party. It is only after he takes them into his own cabin that he realizes they will repay his kindness...with betrayal. When the backshooters reveal their true colors, Nate knows he is in for a brutal battle—with the lives of his family hanging in the balance.

___4399-8 $3.99 US/$4.99 CAN

Dorchester Publishing Co., Inc.
P.O. Box 6640
Wayne, PA 19087-8640

Please add $1.75 for shipping and handling for the first book and $.50 for each book thereafter. NY, NYC, and PA residents, please add appropriate sales tax. No cash, stamps, or C.O.D.s. All orders shipped within 6 weeks via postal service book rate. Canadian orders require $2.00 extra postage and must be paid in U.S. dollars through a U.S. banking facility.

Name_____
Address_____
City_____ State_____ Zip_____
I have enclosed $_____ in payment for the checked book(s).
Payment <u>must</u> accompany all orders. ❏ Please send a free catalog.
CHECK OUT OUR WEBSITE! www.dorchesterpub.com

WILDERNESS

#25
FRONTIER MAYHEM

David Thompson

The unforgiving wilderness of the Rocky Mountains forces a boy to grow up fast, so Nate King taught his son, Zach, how to survive the constant hazards and hardships—and he taught him well. With an Indian war party on the prowl and a marauding grizzly on the loose, young Zach is about to face the test of his life, with no room for failure. But there is one danger Nate hasn't prepared Zach for—a beautiful girl with blue eyes.

___4433-1 $3.99 US/$4.99 CAN

Dorchester Publishing Co., Inc.
P.O. Box 6640
Wayne, PA 19087-8640

Please add $1.75 for shipping and handling for the first book and $.50 for each book thereafter. NY, NYC, and PA residents, please add appropriate sales tax. No cash, stamps, or C.O.D.s. All orders shipped within 6 weeks via postal service book rate. Canadian orders require $2.00 extra postage and must be paid in U.S. dollars through a U.S. banking facility.

Name_____

Address_____

City_____State_____Zip_____

I have enclosed $_____ in payment for the checked book(s).

Payment <u>must</u> accompany all orders. ☐ Please send a free catalog.

CHECK OUT OUR WEBSITE! www.dorchesterpub.com

WILDERNESS

BLOOD FEUD

←——————————————→

David Thompson

The brutal wilderness of the Rocky Mountains can be deadly to those unaccustomed to its dangers. So when a clan of travelers from the hill country back East arrive at Nate King's part of the mountain, Nate is more than willing to lend a hand and show them some hospitality. He has no way of knowing that this clan is used to fighting—and killing—for what they want. And they want Nate's land for their own!

___4477-3 $3.99 US/$4.99 CAN

Dorchester Publishing Co., Inc.
P.O. Box 6640
Wayne, PA 19087-8640

Please add $1.75 for shipping and handling for the first book and $.50 for each book thereafter. NY, NYC, and PA residents, please add appropriate sales tax. No cash, stamps, or C.O.D.s. All orders shipped within 6 weeks via postal service book rate. Canadian orders require $2.00 extra postage and must be paid in U.S. dollars through a U.S. banking facility.

Name_____

Address_____

City_____ State_____ Zip_____

I have enclosed $_____ in payment for the checked book(s).

Payment <u>must</u> accompany all orders. ❑ Please send a free catalog.

CHECK OUT OUR WEBSITE! www.dorchesterpub.com